HELL-CRAZY RANGE

FRANCIS W. HILTON

SAGEBRUSH
Large Print Westerns

First published in the United States by H.C. Kinsey

First Isis Edition
published 2020
by arrangement with
Golden West Literary Agency

*A catalogue record for this book is available
from the British Library.*

ISBN 978–1–78541–857–0

Published by
Ulverscroft Limited
Anstey, Leicestershire

Set by Words & Graphics Ltd.
Anstey, Leicestershire
Printed and bound in Great Britain by
T J. International Ltd., Padstow, Cornwall

This book is printed on acid-free paper

CHAPTER
ONE

"Chuckwallow" Grayson, foreman of the Lazy JP Cattle Company, speared another half peach from a can propped between his knees, swiped a dripping jack-knife on brush-scarred chaps, and squinted up the single, sun-baked street of Bigtrails.

"I wouldn't have dreamed the old range had it in her to go so hell-crazy," he observed, his gray-stubbled face as drab and weatherbeaten as the score of buildings flanking the dilapidated board walks. "We used to have range wars twenty years back ... Don't think we didn't. But they were regular quilting bees stacked up alongside of this one. We had rustlers too ... Wherever there's cows you're going to find rustlers. But in the old days, before the railroad come, there was a limit to the number of head they could get rid of. Butchered beef? Sure. A hellslew of it. But we didn't stand around like a bunch of chickens with their feet froze and wait for sheriffs and other danged fool things. A throw rope and the limb of the first cottonwood we came to was all we needed. That combination had all the kangaroo courts in the world skinned hands down for putting the fear of God into cow thieves."

1

Chuckwallow speared himself another peach and swiped the scraggly gramma grass mustache that drooped like tusks at the corners of his wind-cracked lips.

The day was blistering, insufferable; one of those July days when the sun beats down like a scourge on the prairies of Wyoming. The air was inert, breathless; suffocating with the stench of hot greasewood, sage and fennel. The flats that engird the cow-town in every direction were griddle-hot, radiated heat like the top of a stove; heat that shimmered upward in dancing waves to veil the horizon, wavering, unreal, everchanging.

"Lonesome" Harry Sager, another of the six dusty-garbed Lazy JP riders squatted on their spur rowels on the deserted railroad platform at Bigtrails, lifted a floppy-brimmed hat to wipe moist, sunburned brown hair back from a sweat-beaded brow, and mop a bronze face, deep-pitted by wind and storm.

"Just you wait, Chuckwallow." He choked on an attempt to clear his mouth of peaches in a single gulp. "Those hombres raising all this hell will think a tornado has hit the range when Tobasco comes snorting along ra'ring to twist tails with them." An apologetic note crept into his booming voice. "You don't want to forget that the Old Man's been laid up with the rheumatism . . . That's why we haven't made as good a showing as we used to . . . But you just watch that kid's smoke."

"You tell 'em, Lonesome," agreed "Cactus" Mullins — a stocky, slug-faced fellow — bullfrogging farther back into the strip of shade cast by the wooden water-tank beside the dingy, cinder-scarred station house. "That is, providing Tobasco hasn't changed any. But I'm leary. Easterners come West. Once in a hell of a while they turn into right smart cowhands. But a cow-waddy goes East . . . What happens? He just comes back to the home range with a flock of damned fool notions."

"You're plumb right there, Cactus," admitted "Red" Maloney in a tone of judicial thought, his freckle-splotched red face screwed up against the blinding glare of distant alkali. "But then it isn't every Westerner that goes East who is a gun-toter like Tobasco. Why, that walloper loves the feel of steel . . . Is all the time itchin' for a scrap . . . Hell-raisin' was just naturally born and bred into him. I'm saying — like Lonesome — watch Tobasco's smoke when he gets strung out. You'll see the Lazy JP come to faster than a green bronc with a handful of cockleburrs under the saddle blanket. The minute that jasper hits town hell will start poppin' . . . Just like it used to before he went away or I'm a crazy, box-kneed rannyhan."

The whistle of a locomotive suddenly split the stillness that enveloped the drab little one-story cow-town and beat itself to a hollow whisper out on the endless miles of teeming brush-clotted wastes.

"There she comes!" Chuckwallow got stiffly to his feet to stand on legs bowed almost to the point of deformity. "Now I'll take a *pasear* down along the cars . . . Ride circle on that Tobasco walloper and haze him in. When you see him coming, you fellows r'ar up on your haunches, howling, and cut loose with your smokepoles. Give him a welcome that'll scare the

3

passengers plumb out of ten years of their growth besides waking up these lazy good-for-nothing natives." He shambled away, spur rowels raking the board platform and jangling noisily.

Ignoring the curious, half-frightened glances and anxious whispers that came from the coach windows of the train, as it ground to a halt, the punchers, who a short time before had thundered in on lather-flecked horses, which snorted and plunged at sight of the unpainted, frame buildings, again became absorbed in their peaches.

After Grayson had stamped on past the smoking car, a tall, broad-shouldered youth alighted. Sighting the knot of cowboys beneath the water-tank, he strode toward them.

"You penny-ante, peach-eating lobos!" he shouted, tossing his suitcase unceremoniously into their midst to send the all but empty peach cans flying, "How are you, anyway?"

The punchers leaped to their feet and reached for their guns. But the celebration they had planned as a sequel to the send-off they had given Tobias Pepper when he had departed for law school four years before, was never staged. Instead of the chaparejosed bespurred cow-waddy, with six-gun strapped to his hip, they had known, they now beheld a man dressed in moleskin riding breeches and shining puttees.

"Gawd!" burst hoarsely from the lips of Cactus, as he rammed his unfired Colt forty-five back into its holster. "Just what I was afraid of. He's gone plumb

4

eastern. Believe it or not, he's even wearing — dude pants!"

The dismay in his voice was reflected on the faces of his companions. They stood dumfounded in the presence of this youth, who was one of them, yet was a stranger. Their critical glances swept him from head to toe.

Unchanged were his steady brown eyes and square jaw, a heritage from his father, Jackson Pepper, owner of the Lazy JP; Jackson Pepper who once had ruled the trails of Cowland with iron fists and flashing Colt. The same unruly mop of chestnut hair sprouted from beneath the golf cap set on the back of his head. The leonine build that had made him the rough-and-tumble fighter of the region seemed even more ponderous and formidable. The long tapering fingers, which once drew a gun with the fastest of the lot in rangeland, were still as graceful as a woman's. The magnetic smile on his boyish face was as fascinating as ever. Yet some incomprehensible thing had changed him; something that suddenly found them self-conscious and embarrassed, half-fearful to fire the salute of welcome.

Lonesome broke the uncomfortable silence. He offered his horny hand stiffly.

"Pleased to see you back, Tobias Pepper."

"Pleased to see me back?" The youth mimicked the formal greeting. "Is that the way you old cow nurses say howdy to a man who has been gone for four years? What's eating you all, anyway?"

"Gawd!" groaned Cactus again. "Imagine him — a-sportin' dude britches!" And his plaint carried a note of sincerity that voiced the disappointment on every face.

By this time, Grayson, his ferocious visage, six-gun and jangling spurs having sent several of the more adventurous tourists ducking back into the vestibules of the coaches, strode up. One look at the youth and he too, extended his hand with noticeable reserve.

"What the hell is this — a funeral?" Tobe blurted out. "You'd think I was a horse thief from the cold reception you wallopers are giving me."

"We're kind of . . . Well . . . took back, so to speak," Red stammered, his face flaming. "We were sort of . . . Well . . . sort of . . . you know . . . Expecting to see you rigged up in them batwing chaps of yours and toting a shooting iron . . . Instead you're all . . . decked out in ladies' riding britches!"

"Go to the devil!" Tobe recovered his suitcase and started up the street. "I'm going to get a drink. You're invited. I don't care whether you come or stay. But I'm telling you, I can still lick the fellow who refuses to drink with me."

In spite of the riding breeches and puttees, it was the Tobe they knew speaking; the Tobias Pepper — his father always insisted upon using the brace of names — they had dubbed Tobasco. Rangeland always nicknames those it loves . . . Can be deadly formal with those it hates.

They called him Tobasco for short, the Lazy JP riders had explained to the Old Man. And spelling was the least of rangeland worries. "T-o-b-a-s-c-o" to them was just as good as "T-a-b-a-s-c-o," meant the same thing in their minds, and was easier to connect with Tobias. And, after all, his sobriquet was no hotter than his surname. But in reality it was not the Pepper that had inspired the nickname; it was the fiery temper, the reckless courage, the lightning draw of this youth — whose escapades had silvered the hair of old Jackson Pepper and, finally, had resulted in the boy being bundled off to law school.

A smile quirked the corners of Red's lips, spread over his freckled face.

"Now you're talking sense, you weasel-eyed, hobble-gaited, old hellion!" he exploded. "Those dude pants just make us leary, that's all. But I'll risk a drink with you for old times' sake. Put 'er there." He extended his hand.

"That's better," chuckled Tobe, grasping it in a grip that made the puncher wince. "Now the rest of you . . . Single-foot up here and make your howdies or I'm going to clean up on the whole hoot-owl crew!"

His charming smile and subtle personality, which invited confidence, brought them forward as he called the roll. Red Maloney, Lonesome Harry Sager, Cactus Mullins, "Cateye" Adams, "Rawhide" Peterson, Chuckwallow Grayson. Yet even now, having made the first move toward a restoration of the comradeship of other days, the punchers were visibly ill at ease before this stranger in a garb alien to cowland. A certain mistrust — the mistrust any man of the silent trails feels for his Eastern brother until he proves himself — lurked in their eyes.

Up the one street of Bigtrails, stark in the scorching sun, silent as a tomb in its afternoon torpor, Tobasco led the way, the tight-lipped, uncertain riders trooping behind.

But at the "Goldbug" saloon, into which they crowded, the greeting was far different. Ivor Johnson, the fat grizzled bartender, threw down his towel and came for Tobe with open arms.

"It's on the house!" he bellowed to the idlers about the place. "Let's drink with Tobasco. Gosh-all-hemlocks, kid, I'm tickled to see you! After the run of blear-eyed idiots we've had hunting homesteads lately, you're sure a sight for sore eyes!"

"Homesteaders?" Tobe pumped the bartender's hand cordially. "I can't imagine any homesteaders fool enough to locate on the Chimney Rock range. Where are they coming from?"

"God only knows." Johnson went back behind, retrieved his towel and started caroming glasses and bottles across the polished bar. "They're flocking in here from every direction. They hang around town for a few days . . . Kind of getting the lay of things, I guess . . . Then they pull out. I hear the range is plumb alive with 'em. How they manage to live beats me."

Struck with wonder that the Chimney Rock range had, after a half century, turned mecca for homesteaders — about as popular in a big cow country as an epidemic of hoof and mouth disease — Tobe stood gazing about the old familiar haunt.

The bottles lining the back bar appeared to have been untouched, their labels grown a little more discolored. The glasses, piled tier on tier, were dingier, a few more chips from their lusterless sides. Flanking the bottles on the wall, Ivor's pictures of women in tights and prize-fighters in characteristic poses were frayed of edge, their captions almost torn away with thumbing. Here and there a new one, ripped from the pages of a pink magazine, showed that the connoisseur still took pride in his gallery of art.

Tobasco eagerly let his gaze rove across the room. Stetsons were distributed on nails along the walls. Their owners, with sunburned, unkempt locks falling across furrowed brows, sat hunched over the green-topped tables, spur rowels hooked in the rungs of their chairs. Their shirts, thrown open at the throat, revealed the backs of necks, seamed and burned a deep brown by the prairie sun. Their fingers, which handled the cards with amazing dexterity, were knotted and scarred, and always seemed to hover directly above the butt of a Colt jutting from a holster at the table's rim.

Many of the men he knew. These greeted him affectionately, stamped forward to shake hands. Others, dozing against the wall, brought down tilted chairs with a bang and nodded. Save for four strangers, the men deserted the tables when the youth shouted a second to Johnson's invitation.

Tobe edged near Grayson.

"What's wrong, Chuckwallow?" he asked in an undertone. "There's something here . . . I can feel it . . . What did dad wire me to come home for?" He passed a telegram to the foreman. "It isn't like him to say nothing more than: 'Come at once. Need you bad.'"

"The old man don't only need you — if you haven't changed — but he needs everybody he can get hold of who ain't afraid to scrap," replied Chuckwallow, sizing up the youth with a coldly critical eye as though trying to decide whether or not he could open his heart to this stranger in riding breeches and puttees, as he once had done to the fearless boy in batwing chaps and high-heeled boots. "But I reckon we'd better talk going home. The boys will get windy enough over their liquor . . . Too damned windy. I'll say this much — you've come back to a range that has gone plumb hell-crazy. And they're making your paw like it."

Of that shrewd nature which needs ask few questions but chooses to reason for itself, Tobasco accepted Grayson's cryptic explanation without comment. But the last sentence brought his teeth together with a click. A grimness, like the fighting mask of a pugilist, settled over his face.

"Where are the rest of the boys?" he asked after a time.

"The Lazy JP is just a small spread running six hands now," Grayson growled. "Hard winters, rustlers, range war . . . The hell-crazy . . . They've about got the Old Man down, Tobe."

"Well, Tobasco," Johnson put in, planting fat arms on the bar and leaning close, "how'd you make out with your schooling? What was it we heard about you having trouble the first year you went away?"

"Didn't amount to much." It was plain the youth's mood had changed. His answer was abstracted. "I just couldn't understand that men no longer carried their law on their hip. One thing I did learn that has meant more to me than anything else. That was to hand the other fellow a little the best of it and take what he has to return with a grin. If it doesn't hit too close, laugh it off. If he gets to treading on your toes, and you know you're right, push him off. Let him start the trouble. Stay out of it until he gets to burning your range, raising hell with your stock, and hurting you for cussed orneriness. Then tear loose and finish the thing up right. The law has got to play on your side then — all the time."

The Lazy JP punchers heard him in dismay. Something of a look of pity crossed Chuckwallow's wrinkled face. That Tobasco, who once had plunged headlong into anything and thought afterwards, should be preaching the Golden Rule was beyond his comprehension. And somehow, to every mind, the strange creed he voiced fitted in with the moleskin breeches and puttees.

While the youth was talking, his wandering gaze had come to rest on one of the four who had made no move to come forward. A lithe-limbed man he was, almost as large and muscular as Tobe himself, with a hard-lined, hawk-like face. He remained seated at a poker table, idly thumbing a deck.

"This is everybody's party!" Tobasco said cordially. "Come on pardner, and have a drink!"

Three of the four hesitated, as though waiting for the one to whom the youth addressed his invitation to make a move. But he only shot Tobasco a defiant look and spoke for the group.

"Don't drink!"

"Have some ginger ale then?" Again Tobe was smiling, pleasant.

"I said *we don't drink!*" The fellow rasped out the refusal.

CHAPTER
TWO

Chuckwallow nudged Tobasco with his elbow.

"It's Soapy Stevens, foreman of the Horseshoe outfit," he said in an undertone. "He's new since you left. Crazy like a fox and orn'rier than hell. The others there are strangers. I don't think they're with him. Pass it up . . . Don't start anything until I can wise you up on the whole layout."

"Horseshoe outfit?" Tobasco returned in surprise. "Why that's old Jake Elliot's spread. Jake is the best friend dad and I ever had. Why won't his foreman drink with us?"

"Jake started the range war I was telling you about," Chuckwallow muttered guardedly. "He's been on the outs with your paw for three years. And he's got your old man cornered anyway he turns. This here Stevens bobbed up right after the hell busted loose. Jake made him foreman. Must think the sun comes up and sets in him, for he's turned over the whole works to Stevens. Jake hasn't been off the ranch for months. Me, I always thought Soapy was ram-rodding a spread of gunmen, because they say he's chain lightning with that iron of his. The country is overrun with jaspers who call themselves homesteaders. Homesteaders, hell! Who'd be damn fool enough to homestead in this country? I've got a hunch they're rustlers or trigger-fanners, laying around on pay, waiting for some big flash. Here! Hold on a minute. Remember what you was preaching a minute ago. Let the other fellow —"

But Tobasco had shaken off the restraining hand Grayson dropped to his shoulder. The grimness, which masked his face when he first had heard his father was in trouble, returned to set the muscles bulging at the corners of his jaw. Pinpoints of flame sprang up in his eyes suddenly to coalesce in a cold set gleam.

"What become of Jake's niece, Peggy Elliot?" he ventured, in a voice that now had grown noticeably cool and drawling.

Grayson had expected the question — and dreaded it. The boy and girl had been raised together; had been inseparable companions before he went away. Their interest in one another had been the pride of old Jake Elliot and Jackson Pepper. The country took it matter-of-factly that some day the marriage of Peggy Elliot and young Tobias Pepper would unite the two great ranches.

During the first year of his absence, the girl shared her letters with Jackson Pepper. Then came the break. After that Chuckwallow seldom saw her; they heard of her only through acquaintances in Bigtrails.

"She's still at the ranch," he answered presently. "Growed up now, I hear. She hates the Lazy JP men worse than most folks hate rattlers." He tried to soften the harsh words.

Tobasco shot him an inscrutable look.

"Old Jake Elliot and dad have split after a half century of friendship," he mused grimly, his gaze now darting about the saloon. "And the foreman of the Horseshoe outfit refuses to drink with us. Don't worry about me, Chuckwallow." His eyes flew back to rest on the man.

"I said it was everybody's party!" There was no cordiality now in his invitation. The tone was sinister, challenging.

"I'm not drinking with any hombre in ladies' britches!" retorted the puncher, kicking back his chair, springing up with a quick, cat-like movement and starting forward. "When I drink, it's with men — not dudes!"

The hands of the Lazy JP crew flashed down suddenly to stop, thumbs hooked in cartridge belts near the butts of holstered Colts. From the corner of his eye, Tobasco caught the movement.

"None of that!" he warned. "Our outfit never ganged up on a lone wolf yet, and it isn't going to start now." His curt command sent the cowboys back around to the bar in disgust. Convinced now they were that his city clothes and strange creed had made a coward of him.

But Tobasco smiled insolently into the face of the advancing Stevens. "I beg your pardon if I have offended," he offered quietly. "I guess I didn't realize the change that has come about in this country in the last four years. It used to be an insult for a man to refuse to drink in Bigtrails. But I don't suppose they consider it as such any more."

Fully aware of the hostile glances of his own men, he turned and picked up his glass of liquor.

"It's still an insult!" the Horseshoe foreman snapped out.

Tobasco spun about again. Anger drained his face of blood. His sensitive lips braced in a thin grim line across his teeth.

"You're not the right heft to drink with!" Stevens took another step, halted within arm's length of the youth. "You're built too much like a sheepherder to suit me. And I sure hate woolly wranglers. Then again, your ladies' pants don't pull none too heavy in your favor. I wouldn't drink with a lousy rustling Lazy JP jasper if I never drank!"

Followed a clock-tick of silence; a deadly suffocating silence that keyed men's nerves and clutched at their throats. The tension became almost tangible. Then came a movement; a movement as swift as a flutter of light. Stevens' right hand flashed down to his Colt. The three strangers were on their feet, had followed suit. In that swift breathless instant, with an infinitely keen perception borne of danger, Tobasco stamped indelibly the faces of that trio on his mind. One, he noted, was minus the last two fingers of his gun hand.

The Colts started away. The savage oath Chuckwallow ripped out was a crazy bellow. With amazing speed, the speed of a striking rattler, the old bandy-legged foreman was before them, gun clutched in knuckle-whitened fingers at his hip, ready to fire at the first hostile move.

16

Four Colts froze on the rim of sweaty holsters. Tinkling rowels on feet suddenly edging to safety from the line of fire jarred gratingly on taut nerves. Three men, dumfounded by the speed of Chuckwallow, from whose pursed lips issued hoarse, inarticulate bawls, were moving back, hands lifted to the black-raftered ceiling.

Another clock-tick, awesome, deadly; a clock-tick impregnated with swift tragedy, stark death . . . Then . . .

Tobasco's move, too, was lightning fast. Coordinated muscles jerked with violence. He catapulted forward. As Stevens' hand started away with his gun, Tobe's fist found his jaw in a cracking, sickening crunch. The Horseshoe foreman lurched backwards, crashed through the swinging doors into the street. His half-drawn Colt clattered to the floor, caromed along to come to rest at the youth's feet. He kicked it aside contemptuously, bounded after Stevens, who shook his head like a bull, jerked straight and came lunging back behind a guard of whipcord muscles.

"Take the guns away from those three tinhorns and run them out of town," Tobasco hurled at his men with his old, easy coolness. "Then one of you go up and get the sheriff. I want this walloper arrested for attempted assault. I'll take care of him while you're gone."

Lonesome sprang forward, attempted to shove a Colt into the youth's hand.

"You'll need it," he whispered hoarsely. "Soapy's bad medicine. The best man in the country with his dukes.

For God's sake bust him over the head with this iron if you don't want to plug him."

Tobasco shot the panting puncher a withering glance which sent him slinking back.

"Any damned coward can fight with a gun!" he snorted. "If you fellows didn't pack those arsenals, you'd all be better off." He sidestepped a blow that whistled past his head. "Get the sheriff. From what Chuckwallow says, we're in no position to have any of our men in jail. This fellow started the thing by attempting to draw after he'd insulted me. I want an officer here to see the finish."

His words fell on unbelieving ears. That Tobasco Pepper was appealing for a sheriff during a fracas was as startling to the Lazy JP cowboys as had been his preachment of the Golden Rule. With a muttered curse Lonesome detached himself from the excited circle and started on a run up the street. He had taken but a few steps, when he halted, whirled back. With his old disregard of danger, Tobasco had side-stepped another terrific blow and stripped off his coat.

"I don't want to get any blood on it," Lonesome heard him say as he handed it to sputtering Chuckwallow. "It's too good a piece of cloth to have this boar bleeding on."

Lonesome hugged himself. Even with his dude turn-out, Tobasco was showing flashes of his former self. Forgotten was Lonesome's mission. He twisted a cigarette with shaking fingers and backed over to lean against the building.

18

Stevens was boring in, his hawk-like face twisted with fury, his great shoulders hunched, bulging. Tobasco, too, had gone into action. Two hundred pounds of brawn and muscle. Lonesome slid down the side of the building, squatted on his rowels. Only the short quick drags on his cigaret now gave evidence of nervousness. Only fear that Tobasco would catch sight of him kept him from cheering. For Tobias Pepper, the rough and tumble fighter he had known in other days was hitting, feinting and showing footwork worthy of a prize ring.

Stevens was no mean opponent. He blocked the terrific punches with maddening ease. Tobasco quickly shifted his tactics. Bringing into tense play all his muscular force, he lifted an uppercut from his knees, crossed with his left, connected. Daylight streaked beneath Soapy's feet. He dove backwards, crashed sprawling into the dusty street.

A hoarse yell went up from the punchers, and the few citizens who had braved the scorching heat and eddies of dust to watch the fight.

"Oh, mamma!" Lonesome could hold in no longer. "Did you see that haymaker!" He was bellowing to the world at large. Sound of his own voice jerked him back. He leaped up, took one more look to make sure the prostrate Stevens would not rise, then started leisurely for the jail, lips puckered in a tuneless whistle.

CHAPTER
THREE

The Bigtrail's jail sat at the head of the street.

It was distinctive in that it was the one brick building the town of sun-warped frame and false fronts boasted. Its four small windows were barred. But the bars had been sadly bent by iron-muscled prisoners. Not so much with an idea of escape — there was little need for escape in lawless Bigtrails — but by cowboys, who "run in" to sober up after protracted sprees, had spent their "jolt" by testing their strength on the offending bars.

The Bigtrails jail had little need for bars. It was the brag of Joe Kazen, the sheriff, that he never yet had lost a prisoner — through escape.

A lanky, gangling fellow was Joe, grizzled, weather-beaten, rundown as the cowtown itself. He loved and he hated with equal intensity; a stanch friend, a relentless foe. Determined to the point of bullheadedness. All in all, he was a good officer, single-handed trying to make the unpopular law a force to be reckoned with. If he feared any man it had yet to be discovered. The big pearl-handled forty-five strapped at his hip had reaped its toll of life along the silent trails. There was still fire in his faded blue eyes. But his wits were far slower than his trigger finger. And his aversion for work was well known.

He rested that blistering July afternoon in the cubby-hole office of the jail. He was tilted back in a chair against the bulletin-littered wall, a mop of damp gray hair lying wetly on a corrugated brow, long legs stretched comfortably across a table. His dime-thin rowels gouged its face, already scratched and rimmed with grooves of countless forgotten cigarets. The one article of furniture beside the chair the office boasted was that table which served as a desk, a catch-all for dust-covered mail, and a place where Joe, an inveterate gambler, dealt "stud" and "blackjack" almost every night with his cronies.

He dozed now between lazy slaps at a persistently buzzing fly. A sudden burst of cheering from the street brought him up, blinking wildly. He dragged his feet from the table, arose, yawned and stretched lazily.

At that moment Lonesome ambled up.

"What's all the racket?" Kazen demanded grumpily, rubbing his eyes.

"Fight," Lonesome grinned.

"Who?"

"Couple of men."

"Didn't think it was a span of mules, you jackass!" Kazen found energy enough to snort. "Who are the men?"

"Tobasco and Soapy Stevens."

"Tobasco?" The officer came to with a start. "Tobasco Pepper? Is that walloper back again to torment the life out of me with his scraps?" He rummaged until he located a plug of tobacco in the pocket of his overalls, and twisted off a generous piece with snaggled teeth.

"I allow he'll worry you a heap more than Soapy," was Lonesome's dry comment.

"Why?"

"Soapy isn't feeling so good."

"Is he dead?" There was almost a note of interest now in Kazen's voice.

"Not quite. But he don't know he ain't. He'd be listening to the bullfrogs if it wasn't too dry for bullfrogs in this damned country. Tobasco sent me up here to get you as soon as Stevens started the ruckus."

"I'll bet he did!" the officer blurted out. "What for?"

"To arrest Stevens for assault."

"Hell's bobcats!" Kazen was alive now. His exclamation was explosive. "Why you lyin' . . . Do you mean to stand there and tell me Tobasco Pepper got into a fight and sent for me? Don't try to be funny, Lonesome. You're too thick-headed. You're . . . This here is serious business. If Tobasco is back and scrapping mad, reckon I had better call out the militia. I'm about the only feller he don't want to see."

"I'm telling you straight." Lonesome hunched onto the table, enjoying Kazen's perplexity. "Reckon his schooling has gone to his head. And Joe . . ." His voice vibrated with disgust. ". . . he's sporting dude britches — and puttees!"

"Now I know you're loco." Kazen stamped from the office. Lonesome fell into step beside him. They walked in silence, straining for a glimpse of what lay beyond a mantling cloud of dust outside the Goldbug. When presently it drifted aside for a moment it revealed Stevens lurching to his feet, only to go down again under a smashing left. They broke into a trot.

"Now let's have that drink," they heard Tobasco yell as they came within earshot. "Chuckwallow, there is one Horseshoe jasper who knows he has been whipped. Where are the other three?"

"Reckon they're in South Dakota by now," Johnson chuckled. "That is, if they didn't ride their horses plumb to death in the fifteen minutes they've been gone."

"Mebbeso," conceded Chuckwallow, who had watched the fight with misgivings. "But don't get the idea we won't hear more about it."

Glancing up the street, he caught sight of the sheriff and Lonesome.

"We'd better forget those drinks," he warned quickly. "Here comes the law. Unless you want to go to jail your first day home, we'd better hustle out of town." He turned back to Tobasco who had not moved, followed the youth's gaze to where a pretty girl had stepped from a store, halted for a moment in terror before starting swiftly toward them.

"Did you hear me?" Chuckwallow demanded. "Let's ride before you get all tangled up with the law."

"Ride?" breathed Tobasco, whose eyes had never left the approaching girl. "Without finding out who she is?"

"That's Peggy, old Jake's niece you was asking about," Grayson muttered, keeping a baleful gaze on the sheriff. "You may have licked Stevens. But she'll trim you down to her size if you so much as open your yawp. She came to town with Soapy. I hear they're sweet on each other . . . Aiming to team up I guess." Something cold and hard that suddenly glinted in the youth's eyes checked him. "We'd better high-tail it —" He broke off. "Howdy Joe," he greeted sheepishly as Kazen panted up.

"Well, Joe Kazen!" shouted Tobasco, seizing the officer's hand, his face once again lighted with the winning smile. "I've had a fight. I'm sorry, Joe, but I just had to whip this jasper. He tried to get his gun. I don't carry one any more."

Speechless with surprise, as much at sight of the youth after four years, as by the thoroughness with which he had closed both Stevens' eyes and opened several cuts on his face, Kazen could only stare at him in amazement.

"How long you been in town, Tobasco?" he managed to ask after a time.

"About an hour. Why?"

"You've done right well," the sheriff grunted, his slow-moving faculties sparring for time to collect. "Been home a hour and only had one scrap. Hell, in the old days you'd of had a dozen in that time . . . But I'm sure glad to see you." It was apparent he was torn between real pleasure at the return of the likeable youth and a sense of remissness in his duty. He glanced down at the prostrate Stevens. "Reckon you haven't forgotten any of your old tricks, either. I kind of hate to arrest you . . . It bein' your first day in town and all."

"Arrest me?" Tobe flashed. "You don't mean to say Bigtrails has reached a point where a man can't go into a saloon peaceably and order a drink without some would-be tough walloper, like this, butting in and attempting to assault him? You can see I'm unarmed. His gun is in there on the floor. There were three other jaspers with him who got hostile . . . Johnson and my men ran them out of town."

"Bigtrails hasn't changed a danged bit," Kazen assured him importantly. "She's just the free and easy little city she always was. And I reckon it won't never be said of her that she denied any man the right to drink without being molested. Stevens here toting a gun and you being bare-fisted makes a heap of difference. Seems like even with those odds, you gave him right smart of a trouncing. Soapy has a nasty way of saying and doing things all right. This isn't the first fight he's started by any means. I've warned him good and plenty. Who were the other three?"

"Strangers to me," put in Johnson.

"Like as not some more of those nesters that are overrunning the country," Kazen muttered. "I wish to God I could find out who is bringing them in. They've all got the same story . . . Plenty of homesteads open. A land of milk and honey where you pick top wages off the sagebrush. Got a hunch most of this rustling that has been reported can be traced to some of these fellows who pose as squatters. Come on up to the office, Tobasco, and we'll chew the fat for awhile."

"I'd better be starting for the ranch, Joe. I haven't seen dad yet. I wish when this Stevens comes to, you'd arrest him. I'll appear against him." He grasped the sheriff's hand again, swung on his heel and started to re-enter the Goldbug. The voice of the girl halted him. She was regarding him strangely. Her faculties seemed groping out of terror at recognition of him.

"And I'll swear out a warrant for this man's arrest too, Mr. Kazen," she blazed.

Tobasco's face went white.

"Peggy," he blurted out, offering his hand. "Don't you know me?" In spite of his visible emotion, the old smile played on his lips.

She ignored the outstretched hand with an angry toss of her head.

CHAPTER
FOUR

The words of the angry girl fell like a weight on Tobe's heart. How different, suddenly, everything seemed. For no reason, apparent at the instant, his world was crumbling about his ears. Memories flashed into his mind in kaleidoscopic review ... Memories of childhood; blessed childhood spent with this girl on a peaceful range ... Youth ... Idyllic hours riding together across the Chimney Rock range ...

As a boy he had galloped bareback across the shimmering prairies to meet her astride her tan and white Shetland, rigged up with only a gunny sack and surcingle. Came the day when his father had given him his first saddle — a gaudy, stamped affair with pancake horn and white buckskin strings. He recalled that a calf later had chewed those strings until they were stiff as slivers. Proudly he had ridden forth to show it to Peggy only to find that she too had a new saddle — old Jackson Pepper and Jake Elliot timed their gifts well so that neither should ever be envious of the other.

From pigtails and short trousers they had grown together to the embarrassed, self-conscious age. That is, embarrassed and self-conscious toward others. But never together. Their camaraderie was too sincere, too free; their understanding of each other's joys and griefs too perfect for embarrassment.

They seemed apart from the rest of the world. They knew every silent trail, every crocus bed, every beauty spot on the Chimney Rock range. Occasionally they were allowed even to venture as far as Bigtrails alone to spend an evening with mutual friends.

He had loved her then in a simple, boyish way. As they grew up that simple understanding had blossomed into something deeper, something that hurt him inside and kept him constantly longing for sight of her. She had always been his. Never, since he could remember, had he doubted it. Never had he been given cause to think differently.

Gorgeous sunsets that drenched the prairies with purple haze, glorious sunrises lifting in a fling of fire-yellow over the rim of the flats: picnics in the wooded depths of the Black Hills, fishing jaunts, long hikes together, horseback rides, horse races, target practise that had given him a lightning draw, bred into a love for the feel of cold steel.

Then had come the day when he had ridden away with the round-up . . . A full-fledged horse wrangler. How she had clung to him, pleaded with him to be careful. Then came their first kiss, a few briny tears . . . But he was grown up now . . . was a man . . . the world lay at his feet.

Thought of their reunion on his return from the round-up even yet stung his eyes. It seemed only yesterday. How the years rolled back in flashing pictures . . . fleeting, panoramic . . . like a dying man relives a lifetime in clock-ticks.

Then he had fallen in with a wild set of cowhands . . . had gone in for bronc-busting and rodeos. More frequent had become his trips to town . . . less and less time could he find to devote to Peggy. Yet still, never had he doubted her love for him, nor his for her . . . Youth must have its fling, it is Cowland's way.

He had grown to manhood on the range. Grown into a rowdy, a rough-and-tumble fighter who fought at the drop of a hat for the sheer love of fighting. He crushed men as he crushed outlaw horses with his ponderous weight, his utter fearlessness, his reckless courage. She had pleaded with him, coaxed tearfully, to no avail.

Then had come the parting. Jackson Pepper himself intervened to halt the wayward course. Much as it hurt, the old fellow had cut the youth loose from his rangeland cronies . . . without ado had bundled him up and sent him off to law school.

Once away from the range, Tobe began to realize the depth of his love for Peggy. He missed her terribly, more even than he missed his father. Writing to her daily became almost a religion. Then, as he became acquainted and the newness of things began to have an appeal, his letters arrived weekly. They were filled with strange things . . . glimpses of a world unknown to her. Of things of which she had always dreamed, longed to see . . . Yet her letters were always the same, protesting a simple girlish love, filled with homely little incidents that brought a lump into his throat.

Once he had settled down in his strange surroundings, he had worked hard. He found little time to write to Peggy. He was living in a different world, a world she could not understand. His letters became infrequent, presently to stop altogether. Hers, too, stopped coming . . . just when he couldn't recall. Yet even then he did not doubt either of their loves. Thought of her always stirred a hurt within him. Every girl he met drew a swift comparison. All of them were found wanting. It was a foregone conclusion in his mind that some day they . . .

Still, once he had stopped writing, it seemed impossible to pick up the thread of correspondence. He would wait until he saw her. The things that he had to say would not go down on paper. Some things are best left unwritten.

And now, after four years, they were face to face. He had always known that she was unusually pretty. But never until this moment had he realized her utter loveliness.

From beneath lowered lids he dared a glance at her pretty face, suddenly conscious of the staring eyes about him. Yes, it was the same Peggy, the same Peggy only with four years of womanhood behind her. He had thought her charming when childish waves of angry color swept her face. But now . . . it was so different . . .

And the pinpoints of flame that glinted in her dark eyes . . . He remembered them of old . . . He had noticed them first the day he had dared her to follow him over the rim-rock on the Chimney Rock buttes. She had refused. He had taunted her with cowardice.

She had flown into a rage. He had laughed those pinpoints of fire out of her eyes then. But now . . .

All too vividly he recalled the gesture when she impatiently brushed aside wisps of auburn hair straying across her face, tanned to a deep olive. Many times he had stretched at her feet on some windswept point and seen that hair straying from beneath her broad-brimmed hat to caress a smooth cheek.

And her corduroy-garbed figure, trembling with rage . . . For all her womanhood she was still that little girl he had known — the Peggy of old, but now with a figure rounded and trim. Even the booted foot that tapped the board walk in an angry gesture that he recalled . . . never before had that foot appeared so dainty; the boot, he noticed idly, was fancy-stitched. Short-shanked, gold-inlaid spurs had replaced . . .

"I insist, Joe Kazen, that you arrest this man!"

It was her voice, low and musical, yet with an uncertain quaver, that jerked him violently from his retrospection. Her coldness set the blood to hammering in his temples. His one wild impulse at the moment was to forget the training that had changed his life and plunge back into the mad world of hot-barreled Colts and writhing gun smoke that he loved.

He was barely conscious that he had turned his back upon her.

"Go ahead and arrest me, Joe," he found himself saying in a husky, unnatural voice. "I wanted to get to the ranch as quickly as possible. I don't give a damn now if I never get there. But if you take me, you're taking Stevens too — or I am!"

His words whipped the last vestige of color from the girl's face.

"Why — To —" She almost slipped, but caught herself quickly. "You — can't — arrest — Mr. Stevens," she faltered.

"Oh, yes we can," Tobe shot back brutally. "And that isn't only half of it, we're going to. I have witnesses that he reached for his gun. My men were quicker than his, that's all."

"His men?" scornfully. "He didn't have any men with him to fight his battles."

"He had three wallopers with him who tried to get their Colts," he told her, quiet now, cold as steel. Then for the first time she met his eyes, searching for his meaning, only to bite her lip on the question she started to ask.

"I'm sorry you saw me in a street brawl, Peggy," he said contritely. "I'm willing to take the blame rather than stir up any trouble." She started violently, the color flooded back into her cheeks. "I've heard there is some sort of misunderstanding between the Lazy JP and the Horseshoe. I haven't been here long enough yet to find out what it is all about. But I want you to know at the outset that the Lazy JP has never had any fight with you or Uncle Jake . . . And as long as there is a Pepper connected with the spread it never will have any fight with you."

His apology left her speechless, her black eyes glowing yet momentarily filled with an uncertain light.

"As for assuming the blame for this brawl, Mr. Pepper — forget it," she managed to get out presently with biting emphasis. "We can take care of our end of the misunderstanding without help from the Lazy JP . . . from the law or anything else." Tears hovered on her long lashes. "I — I . . . never mind arresting him, Mr. Kazen," she threw at the gaping officer. "Please get a doctor for Mr. Stevens and have him taken to the hotel." She bent over the prostrate man, who, however, had revived and was peering up at them from swollen eyes.

Tobasco winced. The sheriff suddenly found occasion to blow his nose vigorously, careful though to conceal his twitching mouth behind a huge red bandana he dragged from a hip pocket. The Lazy JP punchers stood rigid, their faces immobile.

The girl helped the groggy Stevens to his feet. Then with flaming face she whirled and flounced across the street, the foreman at her heels. Tobasco watched them until they had disappeared, perplexity and pain in his eyes.

"You're a hell of a walloper to be preaching about staying out of trouble," Lonesome broke the embarrassing silence to snort at the youth's elbow. "You've been in town just long enough to have a fight, have a run-in with a girl, order three strangers to hit the grit, and just miss being arrested. Guess what Peggy said though will hold you plumb peaceful on the bed ground. 'Pears like to me she wasn't just what you'd call tickled to death at knowing who you were. Did you notice it?"

Tobe jerked with muscular violence. He spun about. The fire in his eyes drove the laughter from Lonesome's voice. The cowboy gulped, blinked and sheepishly sidled away.

"Let's light out for the ranch. Round up the boys," Tobe ordered Chuckwallow quietly.

Swinging onto one of the Lazy JP horses tied at the hitch rail in front of the saloon, and shouting for Johnson to take care of his suitcase, he set the pace for the hard-riding crew as it galloped out of town and headed for the grim wilderness of Chimney Rocks, where lay the home ranch.

CHAPTER
FIVE

Once their horses had pushed the village of Bigtrails behind them Tobasco faced the blazing trail with broad shoulders squared, chest expanded, squinted eyes sweeping the limitless expanse that blinded with its glazy brilliance. The sun beat down cruelly to wilt the men in their saddles and drag sweat from heaving flanks.

The arid flats, clotted with greasewood that rose belly-high to a horse, glared white with patches of alkali. Bunchgrass and sedge were seared and buff, burned on the stem by the scourging sun. Delicate gumbo lilies sprinkled the brick-hard earth, peeked from the sheltering shade of the brush as though to prove they could survive the merciless aridity where other vegetation withered and died away.

Ugly, weirdly-shaped buttes stepped away, finally to become but dim etchings in the smoke-blue air. An occasional gnarled cottonwood gave promise of water, a promise that was not fulfilled by the sun-cracked beds of writhing wadies.

Far to the West the Chimney Rocks — huge piles of rim-rocked gumbo — rose sheer from the prairie floor to poke their spiny noses into the coppery heavens, dance like a mirage in the shimmering heat and blend with the horizon, unreal, distorted, everchanging.

To the east a low-hanging murky streak — like smoke on an ocean's rim — showed where the pineclad Black Hills, bristling with crags and gutted by canyons, reared their helms skyward.

The air was heavy with the scent of fennel, sage and greasewood. Dust scuffed up by drumming hoofs rose chokingly from the trail to powder the riders with a thin dry film, glisten in the stubble on lean faces and drift lazily away on the slow hot wind finally to become a deeper layer on dusty brush.

It was a land bereft of beauty, a land griddle-hot, radiating heat like the top of a stove, uninviting, infested with flies and mosquitoes that lay in a blanket along the ponies' sweating necks and flanks. A land devoid of habitation save for stray bunches of bawling cattle — prowling the wastes in search of water — which broke away at their approach to run in half circles and stare back inquisitively. Here and there a lone steer, goaded to frenzy by tormenting flies, horned savagely at the greasewood, or pushed a bleeding jowl across the cactus-spiked ground. An occasional jack bounded away to stop at a safe distance, sit on its haunches and look back. Diamond-backs, stretched full-length, were too comfortable in the sickening heat to dispute their advance.

To the accompaniment of jangling spur rowels, the creak of sticky leather and the rhythmic "thumpity-thumpity" of the hoofs of ponies loping mechanically through the afternoon, Chuckwallow, with noticeable reluctance, unfolded the story of the range war.

"It all happened over one measly steer," the old foreman told Tobasco, as he rode, seat glued to the saddle, arms flapping like the wings of a crane. "Your paw roped it out on the Chimney range. Thinking it was a Lazy JP, the brand being dimlike, he re-ran it. Old Jake came along just then. What does he do but claim the critter. Of course, our old man was snorting and r'aring to go on the prod. They got to chewing the rag for a spell. Jake proved the steer was his, all right. It was the first time in thirty years those two brands — the Lazy JP and the Horseshoe — ever got twisted. Your paw toned down — was all broke up. He offered to give the critter back to Jake or pay him a top price for it. Old Jake, the stubborn old bull-bat, was mad clear to his innards. Claimed he'd been losing a heap of stuff and accused your paw of rustling. You know what that did to the old man? He went hog-wild, fought his head like a dog with a mouth full of porcupine quills. And, being the old man, he went off half-cocked, like he's done all his life.

"That afternoon, some of the Horseshoe men picked Jake up out yonder by the Chimney Rocks. Drilled through the shoulder." Chuckwallow jerked at his gramma mustache and shrugged. "The war was on," he grunted.

Tobasco passed no comment. He stared straight ahead, lips set in a thin grim line across his teeth.

"What has happened so far, Chuckwallow?" he broke his silence after a time.

The foreman's only answer was to shift sidewise in his saddle, throw his weight in one stirrup and regard him critically.

"Quit staring at me like I was a horse thief!" Tobe flashed petulantly. "You make me nervous. What the hell's the matter with you wallopers? Just because I happen to be wearing breeches instead of chaps isn't any reason for you or any other cowhand to mistrust me."

"Mebby not," Grayson conceded dubiously, pushing back his Stetson to run horny fingers through wet gray hair and brush it away from a dripping brow. "But we ain't never got used to women's britches. Then again, there's that fool gospel you was preaching . . . About giving the other feller the edge on things. Mebbeso that might work back East where they don't have range wars and sneaking coyotes and fugitive gunmen. But . . . It ain't worth a damn in a hostile cow country, that's all."

Tobasco turned on him eyes that were heavy with seriousness.

"It will work here just the same as anywhere. There's a mighty bitter experience ahead of you and every other old-timer, Chuckwallow. You've got to learn that there are courts now to settle disputes, instead of forty-fives. And the courts are going to handle this feud."

"Yep," the old cowman snorted disgustedly, jerking straight in his saddle and giving his horse the rowels, "and you'll get all hell whipped out of you trying to get justice in a Bigtrails court if you figure that is the way to fight in Cowland."

"There are courts the fellows who sit on juries in Bigtrails never heard of," Tobasco flung back. "And we'll carry this thing to the highest there is, if we have to. Hard as it is for you to understand, Chuckwallow, you'll find there is nothing too big for the law."

Grayson jabbed his goaded pony to a more savage pace and fell to chewing the ragged ends of his mustache. Skeptical, in spite of the way Tobasco, in breeches and puttees, had acquitted himself with Stevens and won his first tilt with the Horseshoe, the punchers pounded along behind in silence, their eyes, shaded by flopping hat brims, glued to the baked ground or roving idly over the scintillating prairies.

The sun blazed its downward course with maddening slowness. Before it had dropped to the horizon, rowels had ceased to bring whistling snorts and angry sunfishes from the ponies. They moved mechanically, their long strides turned to choppy, back-wrenching jerks of dog-tired legs, caked with the mud of dust and sweat. Utter weariness had put a sag in the shoulders of the punchers. Their faces were streaked with grime.

After an infinity of time the shadows began to lengthen across the brush. A welcome coolness crept into the breeze, breathing life into weary ponies, and lifting hat brims from bloodshot eyes. Then presently the sun had slipped below the skyline in a sea of metal brilliance. All color blended into one . . . Deep purple, hazy, indistinct.

Dusk fell swiftly. It found the group riding out onto the rim of a hogback. Two miles below, the buildings of the Lazy JP lay huddled in the valley.

Tired as he was, Tobasco thrilled to the sight. He pulled rein, stood up in his stirrups. Nothing had changed. The endless plains, the pungent tang of sage, the very air seemed to satisfy a craving that had possessed him for years. The old ranch with its weather-stained cabins, the ends of the logs speckled with staring yellow pitch knots . . . the Chimney Rocks, beyond, cold and austere in the gathering gloom. The divide that separated the sage country from the barrier of hills — somber and black in their cloak of pines — dashed away as nothing else could, the restlessness that had lain heavy on his soul. Yet now there was a new weight come to replace the old . . . Everywhere he looked he seemed to meet the accusing eyes of Peggy Elliot and to see some familiar thing that recalled her vividly to his mind.

Ignoring the impatience of the men, he remained motionless, reveling in the scene. Suddenly his body jerked straight.

Came a rattle of shots!

Grayson went rigid in his stirrups.

"What the hell?" burst from his whitened lips.

The others sat their pawing, bit-champing horses taut, straining ahead. A confused mass had detached itself from the buildings, dropped back from a single gun that was spurting flame into the lowering light.

"They've cornered the old man!" Chuckwallow shouted, lifting his weary mount with the rowels and crowding it down the rocky face of the hogback on its rump. "Unlimber your guns, fellow . . . had a hunch this was coming. It's a showdown now . . ."

CHAPTER
SIX

The men followed the foreman at a reckless pace. Sensing the nervousness of the riders, the horses — now within sight of home and rest — ran madly on tightened reins, taking clumps of brush in great lunges, leaping dry washes, thundering on. They had almost reached the outer gate of the ranch when Tobasco pushed his blowing mount alongside Grayson.

"Don't do anything rash, Chuckwallow," he jerked out. "Find out what it is all about before you start any shooting."

The old foreman muttered something under his breath, but kept his eyes straight ahead.

Warned by the clatter of hoofs of the return of the Lazy JP crew, the confused mass suddenly took shape in the form of three riders. Before the cowboys were near enough for recognition, they threw themselves onto their mounts and raced away in the opposite direction. Unable to give chase on their goaded horses, the punchers dropped the barbed wire gate and thundered up to the ranch-house.

"There's a sample of holding your fire," Grayson broke his ugly silence to snort at Tobasco as he leaped down, dropped the reins and lumbered toward the porch. "We could of dropped one of those damned coyotes . . . He'd of talked on the hondo end of a thirty-foot throw rope."

The youth held his tongue under the withering scorn in the foreman's tone.

Then they were bunched, bounding onto the porch, only to leap back from the muzzle of a Winchester in the hands of a white-faced cook.

"Stand back!" he warned in an incisive, high-pitched voice. "I'll drop you! Don't come a step . . ."

"Shut up!" Chuckwallow barked. "What's wrong?"

"God-a' mighty!" panted the cook, reassured by the voice and lowering his gun. "They've killed the Old Man. Tobasco!" He dropped the Winchester and sprang forward to throw his arms around the youth. "I'm sure glad you got here . . . But God-a'mighty . . . The Old Man was out to the barn when they rode up. Three of 'em . . . Don't know what started the trouble . . . Don't know what it . . . But they shot him down. I seen 'em do that. I ran out and dragged him into the house. But I reckon he's due to cash in his chips."

Tobasco tore from the terrified fellow's arms, and bounded into the adjoining room. His father was stretched on a couch, fighting for breath. A gleam of pleasure lighted the dim eyes at sight of him.

"They got me — Tobias Pepper!" the old cowman gasped.

"Who?" Tobasco dropped on his knees beside the old fellow, gripped a horny hand. "Who did it, Dad?" He fought to control his voice.

42

"Don't know." The old man clung to him frantically. "Didn't recognize a one of them. Three strangers. I pumped it into 'em . . . Ran out of cartridges. I'd of . . ." His voice mounted shrilly. He attempted to rise. The effort was too great. He sank back with a moan.

"What was it about?" Tobasco threw a restraining arm about his shoulders, striving to quiet him a little.

"That state section we've been leasing for the last twenty years. Got my notification the lease would expire in thirty days. Been laid up with rheumatiz . . . couldn't write . . . get to town . . . 'tend to it. Old Jake Elliot . . . The ornery hellion . . . leased it."

"Not the section with the water-holes on it?" Tobe demanded. "But never mind Dad . . . I'll get doc . . ."

"Yep. The Lazy JP ain't got a drop of water now for its stock."

"How do you know Jake leased it?"

"One of them hombres, the one who shot me — let drop a remark. First I'd heard about it. They was old Jake's men sure . . . Or they wouldn't have known it. They got hostile. I tried to hold them off. They were too many for me . . . they . . . started . . . firing . . ."

"Who shot first, dad?" Tobasco gulped.

"Who shot first?" The old fellow lurched up on his elbow by dint of desperation. "Who the hell did you think? I did, of course. Any Pepper who won't cut loose first ain't worth a damn. It's the way I've got along my whole life . . . getting the drop on the other fellow. But . . . God I'm tired . . . It's getting dark —" He sank with a groan. "Ain't no use in going for a doctor. The jig's up —" He fought for the breath that now rasped croupily in his throat. "I'm glad you've come . . . The ranch and everything is yours. Don't forget you're a Pepper. All my papers are yonder in the desk ready for you . . . Been expecting this. The range ain't what it used to be. She's plumb shot to hell. Rustlers thicker than fleas . . ." His voice sank almost to a whisper.

Unashamed of the tears that hovered on his lashes, Tobe clung to the twitching figure. ". . . Nesters flocking in by carloads . . . losing cows in droves . . . Find the hombre — who owns the Circle R . . . I'm . . . Tobias Pepper —" He jerked with muscular violence. "— My last wish . . . Clean out — that — Horseshoe — bunch — if — they — lay — you — in — the — sod — beside — me."

"Dad!" the youth cried in a strained, unnatural voice. "God, Dad, I . . . What did the man look like who shot you?"

The misty eyes opened, roved about for a moment vacantly. The lips moved faintly. "— Two — fingers — missing . . . So long — Tobias Pepper — Tell — the — boys —"

Tobasco swiped at his eyes, choked on the lump that suddenly had come into his throat, groped blindly for the pulse. It had stopped. Slowly he arose, straightened the limp figure, pulled a covering over it and turned away.

"Two fingers missing!" Those last words pounded in his misery-dulled brain. "Two fingers missing!"

As his scattered wits returned there flashed to his mind the scene in the Goldbug saloon . . . The tense deadly silence that had preceded his clash with Soapy.

44

One of the three strangers who had started for their guns . . . He looked up to meet the misty accusing eyes of Chuckwallow and of the rest of the punchers.

"Now where's your courts?" Grayson demanded in a cracked voice. "Now where . . . that damned outfit has killed your paw — our Old Man — got hold of the only water on the place."

Tobasco made no reply. He strode over to the window to stand, sunk in meditation, his gaze wandering over the expanse of murky plain that ran to the Chimney Rocks, now as dark and foreboding as the battle raging within him. For an infinity of time he watched with unseeing eyes then, motioning the others outside, he too quit the room and quietly pulled shut the door behind him and stood forlornly among the men.

"The Old Man's gone," Chuckwallow choked. "It's up to you. There ain't a jasper among us who won't give up the ghost for the Lazy JP. You heard what your paw asked — clean out that Horseshoe bunch if they lay you in the sod beside him; are you going to do it?"

Still Tobasco made no answer. He stood staring mutely at the foreman. He had aged perceptibly. Haggard lines seamed his face. His narrowed lips, the muscles bulging at the corners of his jaws, were evidence of teeth tight-set with emotion.

Chuckwallow, the watching punchers, felt a thrill of exultation. It was the fighting face of the Peppers — ragged, rugged with the indomitable courage that had made the name of Jackson Pepper feared the length and breadth of rangeland.

When finally the youth did speak, his voice lacked the harshness of his father's bark, but the cool metallic tone was far more sinister and deadly.

"No," he said evenly. "I am not going to clean out the Horseshoe outfit like Dad wanted me to. He . . . he wouldn't understand, but — he belonged to the old school — the school of lovable hardheads and roaring six-guns. His methods might have been right at one time; when there was no law; when a man was forced to defend his life, his home . . . But those days are gone forever. I'll whip the Horseshoe to a standstill — if they're behind these things — but I'll never consent to let our men clean them out with lead, unless they carry the feud to a point where we, too, are forced to defend our lives and property!"

Chuckwallow took a step forward, his weatherbeaten face twisted with fury.

"Forced to defend our lives and property," he rasped out contemptuously. "With your paw murdered, do you mean to stand there, you a Pepper, and say you ain't going to do what your poor old paw asked with his last breath?"

"No!" Tobasco bit off the word. "Because there are other ways now, Chuckwallow. I've learned that throwing lead back and forth across a barbed wire fence is not the way to settle arguments such as this."

"I've been with the Old Man come twenty years!" Grayson's voice snapped like a lash. "I've followed him into some of the damnedest mixups ary you heard of. I got the first time ever to see him turn tail. But I can't say the same for you. When I sighted them dude pants

46

and puttees I got leary. You're yaller clean to the bone, that's what you are . . . Yaller, do you hear! Just like all other kid-glove hombres who don't know nothing about the range. As for me, I'm through! Give me my time. I won't work for no damned coward!"

CHAPTER
SEVEN

Seconds ticked by; poignant, deadly seconds without breath or motion. Tobasco was the first to move. His huge frame jerked with a perceptible tremor. A slow pale shade blotted out the tan from his cheeks. Points of flame flecked the depths of his brown eyes, only to become cold shafts. The muscles at the corners of his jaw twitched. His fists clenched until the knuckles stood out bloodless but, at first, no words came to break the silence.

"It's your age and the love I know you had for Dad that keeps me from taking your gun away from you and breaking it over your head, Chuckwallow," he said presently in a voice that had grown metallic, ringing with tension. "My pants and puttees have nothing whatever to do with a thing like this. Clothes don't make the man. You're the first man who ever called me a coward . . . and got away with it. It's only because I appreciate the admirable spirit behind your words that I'll swallow them."

"You take your job and go to hell!" Grayson repeated savagely, his bowed legs spraddled wide, his eyes gleaming balefully through the dusky interior of the room, his right hand fingering the butt of his forty-five.

48

"I'm saying over again — I'm tellin' the whole damned world — no hombre who won't carry out his paw's dying wish is fit to be called a man."

Blinded by fury, the foreman failed to heed the danger signals the others, on edge with fearful expectancy, had seen many times before in Tobasco's eyes. They waited with bated breath, the disgust on their faces showing plainly their sympathies were all with Grayson.

"Everyone has a right to his own opinion." Something of a smile moved Tobasco's lips; a nervous quirking, sinister, unnatural. "But expressing that opinion — sometimes — is — a — mistake!"

Quicker than Chuckwallow's hand, which snatched for the Colt in his holster, Tobasco sprang forward, knocked the forty-five from the foreman's fingers with a snap that all but broke his wrist and sent the gun flying across the room. With scarcely an effort, he lifted the struggling Grayson off his feet, clutched his throat with one mighty hand, and, holding him at arm's length, shook him until he was gasping for breath. Then, slamming him into a corner, Tobe walked across the room, picked up the Colt, and handed it to the dazed Chuckwallow, butt first.

"I could have crushed the life out of you with my naked hands in spite of your gun," he said, fighting to keep his voice even. "But I wouldn't know what to do around here without you. And get this . . . I wouldn't give you your time on a bet. If you're the friend of Dad's you profess to be, you'll be my friend now when I need you. And that goes for every one of you. I want you to stay. If you haven't enough loyalty to stick with me, I'll stake you and give you your pick of any horse on the place to leave. But let me warn you all. Hereafter, no matter what you think of Tobias Pepper, be damned sure you keep it to yourself!" Wheeling, he strode from the room, leaving the dumfounded crew staring after him.

Supper that evening at the Lazy JP was a dismal affair. Having dispatched Lonesome Harry — the one man in the entire crew of whose friendship he felt certain — to town for the coroner and the sheriff, Tobasco ate in glum silence. While none of the punchers looked at him directly, he could feel their furtive glances as he bent over his plate struggling to down the tasteless food. Grayson was sullen, slamming things about pettishly, apparently bent on drawing the youth into an argument which could be used as an excuse to reopen the affair of an hour before. But Tobasco paid no attention to him, which only served to increase Grayson's rage as the meal progressed.

The shock of his father's death, Peggy's coldness, the rush of events which had poured in upon him, had left the youth's mind in a jumble. Time and again he was tempted to recede from the stand he had taken, tempted to seize the gauntlet the Horseshoe had thrown down, and turn his men loose to settle the feud with flaming lead. But four years of training in a different world had instilled within him a strain of caution. Where once he would have plunged headlong into the fight, trusting to luck and good aim to pull him

50

through, his movements now were guided by a cold, hard reason destined to obtain results far more deadly in their effect than a fusillade of random shots.

Nauseated by the food, which seemed to stick in his throat, he got to his feet and strolled, bare-headed, into the balmy night. Determined to reach a more agreeable understanding, Chuckwallow too quit the table abruptly and followed. Fully aware of the resentment smouldering within the foreman, the others exchanged meaning glances but sat tense, waiting for the report of a Colt they all believed would come. It was Cowland's way.

Tobasco walked slowly past the round corrals, the barns, and moved on toward the lower gate. A full moon hung like a gigantic lantern in the east, drenching the prairies with a silver haze. Greasewood and sage loomed out of the gloom, like hideous monsters of a nightmare, huge, misshapen. The night was filled with noise; the thin whispering chirp of a cricket, bullfrogs croaking in the distant water-holes, zooming bullbats, the plaintive cry of the phoebe-bird. Out of the far dark from below came the measured challenge of a steer to be caught up above and hurled back into the night. Somewhere a coyote set up a yapping, that sounded like a dozen, ended in a long-drawn quavering wail.

All these sounds, a part of the prairie, noisy to the untuned ear, awesomely quiet and peaceful to the rangeland folk, twanged a responsive chord within Tobasco. Yet strangely, that very quiet warmed his blood, made him savagely eager to strap on his gun and avenge his father's death. But back of the wild impulse was cold reason; reason that rose as an insurmountable barrier to rash and reckless judgment.

Instead of jumping at conclusions as he once had done, as he now was prompted to do, he found himself weighing the thing carefully in his mind. Of the group in the saloon that had witnessed the fight, he believed he was the only one who had snapped the mental image of the man minus two fingers from his gun hand. His father's dying words — that the slayer had two fingers missing — was the clue upon which he hoped to sift the murder to the bottom.

Beyond question the killer was one of the three strangers who had leaped to the defense of Soapy Stevens at the Goldbug. That the man knew of Elliot's lease of the Lazy JP state section, on the face of it, stamped him as a Horseshoe employee. Yet Peggy had denied that Stevens had any of his men in town with him. He wondered what his father had meant by asking him to find the owner of the Circle R? This he resolved to ask Chuckwallow at the first opportunity.

His thoughts ran riot, pivoted like a whirligig. Now before him flashed the ashen face of his father. Now the face of Peggy as he had seen her, as he had hoped to see her . . . a part of the familiar surroundings, a part of the peaceful night. He ground his teeth on the dream, walked on sunk in thought that took no notice of time or distance.

"I can't do it, Dad," he found himself muttering aloud. "I've had a new creed pounded into me. You'd never understand any more than Chuckwallow did, I know, but —" He broke off abruptly, listening. His ear, trained since childhood to every sound of the range, had caught a sound; a faint alien sound like that of a stealthy footfall. It was too early for Lonesome to be returning from town. The others were still at supper. A quick survey of the moon-drenched flats revealed nothing. Deciding presently he had been mistaken, he strolled on again, quickly to be lost in his hopeless, endless musings.

He had gone but a short distance when that unexplainable sense of impending danger that makes a man sidestep brush beneath which coils a rattlesnake, tightened his nerves, brought him whirling about to drop to the ground.

A bullet smashed out from the darkness behind, went "pinging" away over his head. The song of hate it sang turned his soul to ice. Rigid, he lay for a breathless moment, stretched full length. Then he raised up his head cautiously and peered about.

The shot brought the punchers tumbling out from the house. Below the gate Tobasco thought he could hear the thud of a pony's hoofs. But he was not positive.

Suddenly a shadowed form, not ten feet away, was revealed in the moonlight. Throwing caution aside, Tobasco bolted to his feet. He bounded forward only to stop stock-still.

The figure was that of Grayson!

"Chuckwallow!" He uttered the name incredulously.

"Who fired that shot?" the foreman blurted out nervously.

Tobasco took firm hold upon himself. His first impulse was to crush the life from the old cowman, who, manifestly, smarting under the affair in the ranch-house had turned stalking assassin to seek revenge. Calm reason rallied to direct his judgment. The others came running up; the sound of awkward feet and the noisy jangle of spur rowels almost drowning the thud of galloping hoofs which Tobasco's quick ear now distinctly caught in the distance.

The punchers, taking in the situation at a glance, halted abruptly. Nervous glances passed between them. It was plain that they momentarily expected the youth to fly into a rage as he once would have done. They did not question who had fired the shot. They had expected it.

Then a strange thing happened. Instead of calling to account the foreman, who stood unperturbed before their accusing eyes, Tobasco whirled on the staring group.

"Red," he snapped out, "bring me the night horse. And stake me to some spurs."

Obviously glad of the chance to escape, Maloney bolted away to obey the command. The others waited tense and breathless for the outburst. But to their amazement it never came. The youth prowled about restlessly until the puncher returned with the night horse. Then he buckled on the spurs and swung into the saddle.

"If I'm not back in a day or two, put the sheriff on my trail." That was all. Before they could offer any protest against him riding forth unarmed, Tobasco lifted the horse into a pounding lope and raced into the night.

"The damn . . . he ain't even packing a gun," Grayson blurted out in a hollow voice. "Here, one of you fellows shag it down to the south pasture and run in the remuda. We'll have to follow that fool with his crazy notions . . . if for no other reason, because he's the old man's kid."

Maloney faced him fearlessly. "Reckon the drubbing he gave you this evening got under your hide just plenty deep, Chuckwallow," he shot at the foreman. "And from what I've seen of him in action, you're damned lucky he didn't tromp all the hell out of you here just now. We've been friends for a long spell. But I'm telling you . . . There'll be no shooting where the galluses cross, or plugging jaspers who ain't armed while Red Maloney is alive and able to go for his iron."

Chuckwallow met his accusing gaze frankly. "I didn't shoot at him," he defended hotly.

"You'd have a hard time trying to convince a court of that," Red threw back.

"It does look suspicious," the foreman admitted. "But honest to God, I didn't fire that shot, Red. Lookee! Here's my gun. Is there an exploded cartridge in it? Smell it? Has it just been shot?"

Red broke the cylinder of the proffered forty-five. The chamber was full. He took a whiff of the barrel. Then he passed the Colt back. An awkwardly embarrassed silence descended upon them. They stood around for a time each busy with his own thoughts. Then out of the far dark came bellowed curses. The drum of running hoofs, the snorts, nickers and squeals of the playful remuda thundering in from the pasture. In utter silence they trooped over to the corral.

Considerable time was lost in corralling the cavvy afoot. The recalcitrant horses, feigning stark terror, bolted past the lowered poles time and again. Once clear of the shouting, cursing punchers, they would wheel to look back as though filled with amazement at the procedure. But before the cowboy shambled in from the pasture the brutes were corralled and a mount roped out. Saddles were secured from the pole rack alongside the corral and hoisted aboard.

Red Maloney stopped with his saddle halfway onto a snaky, twisting back.

"Well, if you didn't try to plug him, Chuckwallow," he said drily, "you're sure lucky it was Tobasco instead of me who caught you snooping around just at the time when that shot was fired. I'd of sifted your old carcass plumb full of holes just on general principles. You can laugh at his new-fangled ideas all you want to. But me, I'm for any jasper who can stand up under gunfire like he just did and not open his chops to the walloper he thinks did the shooting.

"You're skating on thin ice, old-timer. And if you'll take a fool's advice, you'll play up to Tobasco; admit that shooting, smoke the pipe of peace, and try and get him to forget it. Those eyes of his have got a God-awful blood color to 'em when he's sore. It's all Pepper. There's no telling when he'll go on the war path, dude pants and all, and just naturally mop up this whole range like he used to."

He succeeded in getting his saddle aboard the lunging pony. He kicked the wind from the swollen belly, and dragged the latigo to the last notch while it nipped at him savagely. Then he swung aboard.

"I'm telling you fellows straight," he announced after the rest of the cowboys had finished rigging up their ponies, and had mounted and headed toward the gate. "That kid's got guts to spare. Nothin' surer than that. Me, from now on I'm sitting into his game." He glared through the gloom at Chuckwallow. "And I'm telling the whole world it's got me to whip when it lights in on Tobasco, dude pants and all!"

CHAPTER
EIGHT

Back again on the hogback overlooking the ranch, Tobe pulled rein on his blowing mount and sat sweeping the moon-sprayed flats. He could hear the running hoofs at the ranch; caught bellowed curses. Ahead, at some distance, he could make out three moving forms on the chalk-white road. Sight of them set him in swift motion. Swinging in a detour to intercept the forms, riders he knew them to be, he galloped down the slope. A short time later he rode into the trail. But the men apparently had changed their course for they had disappeared. Only a drumming of hoofs so far away it was but a throb on the night air and might have come from any direction, broke the piercing stillness.

"There's one shooting that can't be laid to the Horseshoe," he mused aloud. "Unless those jaspers don't intend to be caught going home." Dismissing from his mind thought of further pursuit, he strained listening until the hoofbeats had become a part of the noise of the night.

Then he went back to his survey of the prairies. Two miles to the west the lights of the Horseshoe ranch were visible. He sat his mount watching them, steady shafts piercing the gloom.

"Do you suppose old Jake Elliot is behind all this?" he asked himself. "Or is there a gang of rustlers working under cover to take advantage of the misunderstanding?"

But with no answer forthcoming, he quickly dismissed the query. Upset by his father's death and the shot from the darkness, heart heavy at the reception Peggy had given him, he rode forward, plunged into thought which took no notice of distance. Before he realized his course, his horse had stopped at the lane running up to the Horseshoe ranch-house. He hesitated for a moment, undecided. Then, prompted by a reckless impulse he was powerless to resist, he dismounted, took down the wire gate and led his pony inside. Swinging up, he rode slowly toward the cluster of buildings. No one was visible around the yard. From the bunkhouses came subdued voices. Riding directly to the porch of the rambling old two-story dwelling, he swung down and knocked.

A riot of mixed feelings possessed him. Suppose . . . Peggy herself opened the door. She drew back startled at sight of him. The color mounted to her forehead and temples.

"I'd like to speak to your uncle," he said quickly in a strained voice. "— on business."

"You'll have to do your business with Mr. Stevens," she told him coldly. "Uncle Jake is —" She stopped. He waited for her to finish, but she did not.

"I don't want to talk to Stevens." He tried to capture her gaze. But it eluded him. "My business is with your uncle. If you have forgotten — to such an extent that

59

you will not ask me in, I wish you would call him to the door."

His heart leaped at the look which flashed across, her face — joy, and fear intermingled.

"Won't you — won't you come in?" she faltered.

Once inside he stood awkwardly, gazing at the old familiar surroundings. The long living room, with a great rough-hewn native stone fireplace, its pine-beamed ceiling blackened by roaring pitch logs. Pretty chintz curtains hung at the windows — a woman's touch everywhere — the massive old furniture . . . vivid recollections assailed him.

He turned presently to the plainly nervous girl who had closed the door and backed against it, one hand clutching her breast to watch him from beneath lowered lids.

"Peggy!" he asked in a husky voice, "what is this all about? What have I done that you should . . ."

"Please, Mr. Pepper," she interrupted, "remember we are — not children any longer." She crossed the room and sank down onto a huge fireside couch. He followed to stand looking down at her, stricken with the thought that she had ceased to care; had forgotten the childish comradeship which was still his sweetest memory.

"All right, Peggy," he said resignedly, after a time. "I won't bother you. I thought at one time you . . ." He stumbled on the word. "I lived for your letters while I was away. Then you stopped writing and —" He fell to pacing about, prey to heart-swelling emotion. "— I never understood it. I knew nothing of this — trouble

— between our outfits until today. I had looked forward to our meeting, to a ride across the flats with you, to a renewal of our — friendship. It was the greatest thing in my life. I longed to come back, to see you once more. And now —" He halted before her; studied her bowed head. The eyes she raised presently glistened with tears.

"Don't, Tobe," she pleaded in a tone from which all coldness had fled. "It will . . . Oh, it's all so terrible . . . it breaks my heart . . ."

"Then you do love me still?" he cried, seizing her roughly by the shoulders.

"Tobe, please!" she pleaded, choking back a sob. "Things can never be the same. I can't explain . . . I . . ."

"They can," he whispered. "I love you, Peggy . . . I've loved you since you were a kid in curls. I want you to marry me . . ."

He beheld in astonishment the change which came over her.

"No," she said, the old coldness in her voice plainly forced. "Please don't ask. It can never be — now. Won't you go?"

Her words stunned him. "I'm sorry," he murmured contritely. "If you'll call your uncle, I'll attend to my business and . . . I won't bother you — again."

He thrilled at the gasp which escaped her tightset lips.

"Oh, Tobe!" There was abject misery in her eyes. "I wish I could tell you everything. But — I — can't."

"Why?" he demanded.

"Because . . . I'm afraid."

"Won't you meet me at the Chimney Rocks tomorrow like you used to when we were kids?" he pleaded. "We could talk again —"

"I — can't," she choked. "You don't understand. Oh, Tobe . . . Uncle Jake — isn't — here any more."

"Isn't here any more?" he asked blankly. "Where is he?"

"He's . . . he's dead."

"Dead?" Tobe flashed in astonishment.

"Oh, please don't repeat it!" she cried in fright. "I should never have told. He would —" She caught herself sharply. But not before a telltale color had flamed in her cheeks.

"Who would?" he demanded, grasping her by the arm. "Peggy, what are you talking about? You're half frightened to death. Who is it? Tell me about your Uncle Jake?"

"You'll never tell?" she swore him to secrecy in a tiny whisper. "He died back East two years ago. I . . . we sent him there after he had trouble with — your father. No one around here knows anything about it. I . . . we decided to keep it secret . . . on account of his enemies. He was buried at his old home . . . in the East."

"I'm sorry, Peggy," he told her sincerely. "I, too, have had my grief. Dad — died tonight."

"Tobe!" she gasped in a pitiful voice. "What — was the matter?"

"Murdered!" he flared savagely. "Shot down on his own ranch by three strangers." A sinister gleam lighted his eyes. His big hands opened and closed convulsively.

"The man who killed him mentioned the Horseshoe lease of the old Lazy JP state section."

"What do you mean?" she faltered, wide-eyed with puzzlement.

"Just what I said," he blurted out, watching her face. "The Horseshoe has leased every water-hole on our ranch. Our cattle haven't a drop."

"There must be some mistake," she cried. "I know of no lease."

"Who owns this place since Uncle Jake died?" he asked.

Again the color surged to her temples, receded to leave her pale.

"Why, I do . . ." she stammered. "That is — Mr. Stevens and I do. You see . . ." She avoided his gaze and rushed on as though anxious to rid herself of some terrible load. ". . . After Uncle Jake died, there was a will. They sent it back to . . . from where he was buried. It gave the ranch to me, a half interest, along with Mr. Stevens." The obvious terror that was racking her sent a dull throb through him.

"Don't cry, Peggy," he pleaded. "It isn't like you. I can't bear to see you unhappy . . . I . . ." Before he scarcely realized what he was about he had pulled her to her feet, swept her into his arms, and was embracing her roughly. For a moment she struggled in his clasp. Then, with a little sigh she laid her tear-stained face against his chest. The blood started pounding wildly in his veins.

"Please — don't — Tobe," she whispered, straining away from him half-heartedly. "You — we have no right . . . I . . ."

"Peggy . . . I love you!" The almost pleading note in her voice, her feeble resistance filled him with an overwhelming sense of joy. He placed a hand beneath her chin, raised her face, bent low to kiss her trembling lips.

"Take your hands off my wife!"

Tobe started violently, spun about, prey to a nameless dread by the ringing command. The girl tore herself from his arms to lean panting against the wall, transfixed by fear and horror. Standing just inside the door, which neither had heard open, was Soapy Stevens, his face evil and twisted with fury. A forty-five dangled in his hand.

Tobasco's head was in a whirl. He dared a glance at Peggy. She refused obstinately to meet his gaze. Nor did she offer any denial of the foreman's claim.

"Peggy!" Tobe's voice was husky with emotion. "Is . . . is it true?"

Minutes passed; tense, throbbing minutes pregnant with a possibility of swift tragedy. Then the girl stirred; a movement lethargic as though she was groping in the haze of a nightmare. But her head nodded in affirmation.

Tobasco suddenly felt the world sliding out from under him. A dismal sense of defeat assailed him; a sickening sense that turned his soul to ice with its awful chill. To his mind flew a grim thought. What a fitting blow to crown the staggering events that had tumbled down upon him with such amazing rapidity in the few short hours since his return to Bigtrails.

His gaze darted back to Stevens. The deadly portent of the moment steadied him. But only for an instant. The foreman's arrogant attitude, the sneer on his weather-cracked lips, suddenly loosed within Tobe all the insane rage that once had been his master. A hazy red mantle, that he had not seen for four years, was slipping before his eyes, goading him to the cold and reckless fury of a maddened bull. With a mighty effort he controlled his voice.

"I didn't know," he flung at Stevens. "I offer my apology." That was all. Manifest repentance, but rasped out in a tone that rang with challenge.

Stevens stood spread-legged, frigid, domineering, hateful, his strange blue eyes, shot with cruel flame, whipping the youth as though seeking some opening through which to pierce his madly working mind. And what he saw set taut muscles to bulging, warned him that any move must be lightning swift, deadly and brooking no mistake.

Tobasco's gaze swept upward from mud-splattered, booted feet, finally to come to rest on Stevens' ugly face. He too, saw something that strung his singing nerves even tighter. He read in Stevens the depth, the recklessly courageous cunning of a man who had faced death and tasted the rawest of rangeland life.

The pantomime continued for moments that seemed like eternities; the unarmed youth staring fearlessly into the hard-lined face of Stevens, his very look daring him on to do his worst.

The foreman was the first to move. A slow pale shade began to blot the tan from his cheeks.

"You expect me to swallow a line like that?" he sneered.

The venom in his tone stung the terrified Peggy back to consciousness of the things going on about her. She sprang forward.

"It's true," she screamed. "He didn't know . . . I didn't tell him . . . We were children together . . . Don't . . . For God's sake . . ." Her words ended in a choking sob.

The muzzle of Soapy's gun, now clutched in a white-knuckled hand at his hip, had suddenly tilted up. A streak of powder flame laced the room. The ceaseless echoes of its report crashed down upon her ringing ears. She peered through the cloud of acrid blue smoke eddying ceiling-ward. Tobe had lurched backwards, thrown up his arms and pitched forward on his face. With an inarticulate cry Peggy sank to her knees beside him.

She was only vaguely conscious of the cowboys coming on a run from the bunkhouse. Then of Stevens' cool voice as he turned them back with word that the discharge had been accidental; that no one was hurt.

The lie stung her to fury; loosed a hatred that gave new strength to her fear-numbed muscles. "You've killed him! You've killed him! You beast! Oh, how I hate you!" she cried. "Tobe! Tobe!" She was clawing frantically at the still figure of the youth stretched on the floor. She searched for the wound, but in her excitement could not locate it. She lifted a face livid with anger to Stevens, who had sheathed his gun and stood leering down at her in cold malice.

"Help me move him to the couch," she choked. "If he's dead —"

Soapy laughed harshly. "You've sure give your hand away," he sneered. "Sometimes it takes a killing to uncover things a fellow would never know otherwise." He pushed her aside roughly and stooped. "I ain't helping this jasper you love for you nor him . . . It's just because, like he told me once, things around here are too good to have him bleeding on!"

She cowered back under his brutal words, stared at him dully as he placed his hands beneath Tobasco's arms, jerked him up roughly and started dragging him across the room.

Then, before her bewildered eyes, something happened with a speed that set her muddled brain to reeling. The suddenness of the thing, the wild hope battling with violent fear within her, drove her to the verge of collapse. She recalled dully hearing a crunching blow, a muttered oath, a heavy thud. She was conscious of being lifted up gently, stretched out full length. Someone was bending over her. She opened her eyes, started up wildly. She was on the couch. Tobe was kneeling at her side.

"You're not dead?" she managed to get out from lips that felt cold and drawn.

"Not yet," he panted. "He just grazed my arm." He showed her a rent in his shirt sleeve and a wound so slight it was scarcely bleeding. "I put on a show to spar for time. I had to play possum. I didn't have a gun. But now . . . He's down for the count. Peggy! Peggy!" She closed her eyes contentedly under the caress in his voice. "I love you more than ever. Why did you do it? Do . . . do you care for him?"

"No!" She sobbed brokenly. "I hate him. I've always loved you, Tobe. I . . . I had no alternative. I had to marry him — or lose my interest in the ranch. That . . . that would have left me penniless, without a — home. Then he . . . he threatened me if I didn't. I despise him. I never let him come near me. He lives with the men down at the bunkhouse. I have been afraid of him ever since the day we — were — married. Tobe! I'm just the same Peggy! I'm yours like I've always been. Please . . . Take me away!" She threw her arms about his neck, buried her flaming face on his shoulder and clung to him desperately.

"I can't, Peggy!" he muttered grimly. "You're his wife. It's — against the law. We wouldn't be happy, that way. But there'll be a way. Be careful. You'll hear from me. I'm going to take up the feud . . . But Peggy, remember always — it's not against you!"

He gently removed her arms from about him, kissed her tenderly. She closed her eyes on the caress. A moment of silence. She looked up. He was gone. She could hear his footsteps on the porch. Then the thunder of a racing pony's hoofs.

She sat up, stared around. Stevens was showing signs of life. Arising, she went to the door, opened it and called the cowboys. With no word of explanation to them when they came in she had them carry the unconscious Stevens to the bunkhouse. Then quitting the living room, she slowly climbed the stairs. Locking herself in her bedroom, she threw herself before an open window and buried her head in outflung arms. For an infinity of time she cried softly. Then she straightened up; and stared through tear-dimmed eyes out onto the moonlit prairies. Somewhere a steer was bellowing a challenge into the night. Like an echo came back an answering bawl. Far down in the Chimney Rock brakes an owl set up a dismal eerie "hoot! hoot!" Out of the far dark a lone coyote began its infernal "yapping," that jarred gratingly on overwrought nerves. She shuddered, and straightened up to throw herself on her bed and lie for endless hours staring up into the gloom.

CHAPTER
NINE

Once off the porch of the Horseshoe ranch-house, Tobasco threw himself into the saddle and rode leisurely to the outer gate. After he had dropped it and remounted he lifted his pony into a pounding lope, with slashing rowels, and headed into the night. The action of a swift horse seemed necessary to the whirling of his mind. Even the winding trail, a chalky ribbon in the moonlight, was indistinct to eyes still hazy with a filament of red. The acrid smell of gunsmoke that still clung to them made his nostrils quiver. He fought valiantly against a wild and reckless impulse that consumed him; an impulse to return to the Lazy JP, strap on his forty-five, ride back to the Horseshoe and defy the whole crew.

The cool breeze whipping his ringing ears, the solemn stillness of the silver-drenched flats eased the tumult in his soul and gradually brought order to his chaotic thoughts. Slowly he gained the upper hand on his rebellious and riotous emotions; was almost calm when, of a sudden, he rounded a butte. Directly below, in a dry wash, the moonlight revealed a group of punchers. He recognized them as they bounded to their feet, hands on their guns. They were the Lazy JP cowboys. He jerked his mount to a gravel-flinging halt among them.

"What's up?" he demanded.

"We followed you in case you needed help," Chuckwallow answered for the group whose hands had left their guns at sound of his voice. "And we run onto a couple of carcasses." He pointed to two freshly-killed steers. The others stood watching, obviously still fearful of trouble between the two. But the shooting at the ranch might never have occurred for any reference Tobasco made to it.

"Nosed around further," Chuckwallow continued. "Found the hides." At his feet were spread two hides with the Lazy JP visible in the moonlight. "They probably seen us coming and didn't have time to bury them deep."

Tobasco ran his fingers through his hair. He appeared to pay no heed to Grayson's words.

"What outfit is the Circle R, Chuckwallow?" he asked quietly.

The foreman plainly was at a loss to answer the question. "It's a new spread come in here about a year after you left," he essayed presently. "They got hold of several sections south of the ranch — down yonder in the lower hills. Nobody knows who they are, nor nothing about them. Don't even know who is running the spread. Some say a stranger. Some say your paw; others say old Jake Elliot; then again I've heard Stevens was mixed up with them. But the truth of it is nobody knows who pays the crew. There's some hard wallopers down there — teased snakes and none too friendly. The ranch-houses lay well back out of sight in the timber — pretty sizeable spread — And you run across just plenty of critters packing that Circle R."

Tobasco shifted sidewise in his saddle to gaze about ponderingly.

"Roll those hides in a slicker so my pony will pack them, Chuckwallow," he ordered after a time. "A couple of you fellows lope along to the house and bring out your bedrolls. Camp here by these carcasses to keep the coyotes and wolves off them until we can turn the whole thing over to Kazen."

"Do you mean to say you're going to let the sheriff handle this out and out case of beef killing?" Chuckwallow blurted out in amazement. "Why man, they've been stringing wallopers up on this range and every other one, for that ever since the Injuns quit the flats."

Another breathless moment for the punchers, who expected Tobasco to call Chuckwallow to account. But still he made no reference to the shooting.

"The Lazy JP has quit stringing men up," he replied shortly. "The code has changed since you were a boy, Chuckwallow! Here . . ." To the men. ". . . I'm playing a hunch that I hope will end this thing pronto. From this minute on I want everyone of you to try to find out who owns the Circle R. I've learned some things tonight that none of you know." Now the cowboys were certain that the break was coming. Even Chuckwallow shifted uneasily. But Tobasco's next words startled them more. "I've been over to the Horseshoe talking with Peggy — and Stevens."

72

"You've been where?" Grayson asked incredulously.

"Over to the Horseshoe ranch."

"Why . . . You didn't have no gun!" the foreman gasped.

"That's what I'm trying to tell you fellows," Tobasco flung back. "If you go around packing your forty-fives and reaching for them every time a man looks cross-eyed at you, of course you're going to get plenty of chances to use them. But if you don't carry one, you seldom, if ever, have need of it."

Manifestly they could not understand this code so strange to cowland. Grayson shook his head dubiously.

"I'll tote my iron when I'm on Horseshoe range," he announced grimly.

Wondering why the youth was deliberately delaying the showdown with the foreman, yet reassured by the attitude of Chuckwallow, who, it was plain, had swallowed his anger and was doing his utmost to be agreeable, the punchers waited for Tobasco's answer.

"I'm not asking you to hang up your Colt," he assured the old cowman. "I'm saying that I want you to be positive you're right before you use it. As far as I'm concerned, I'm not carrying one any more." He swung down and wrapped a bridle rein about a clump of brush, then he strode among them, dropped crosslegged onto the ground, twisted a cigaret and inhaled a deep drag which he expelled quickly through his nostrils.

"Let me spill you fellows a windy while we're waiting for the boys." He settled back on one elbow, spoke quietly, musingly.

"When I went to college, I hit town all rigged up in my Sunday layout: chaps, Stetson, and high-heeled boots. Of course, I didn't take off my gun. I must have been a funny-looking object, although it didn't dawn on me until six months later, that I seemed funny to the other students. I was green — greener than any grassfed yearling we ever had on the Chimney Rock. I sunburned the roof of my mouth looking up at the buildings. I danged near run myself down dodging the contraptions on wheels in the streets. But I finally managed to locate a hotel. Then I started out to buy everyone a drink. Couldn't get a soul to move up to the bar with me. That made me sore.

"Figuring it was my clothes, I toned down, stashed my forty-five, and collected a flock of city duds. They seemed pretty tame after goat-hair chaps and red silk shirts, but I guess they were about as loud as could be bought. After that, I found it was easy to make acquaintances among the Easterners.

"But I couldn't get used to shoes. So I wore my boots. The first day I got on my feet to recite I was scared as that wild bunch that used to run over on Boxelder. I stammered and got tongue-tied until somebody bleated like a sheep. That kind of steadied me. I ripped my book in two, tromped it on the floor, quit that classroom on a high lope and headed back to the hotel. I fished the old Colt out of my truck and high-tailed it back to the law building. I took up herd duty just outside the door.

"By and by, the wise jaspers who liked to bleat like sheep started out. I didn't want to kill them, so I just

74

rapped them over the head with the butt of my gun as easy as I could.

"Hadn't dropped more than eight or ten when the professor put in a riot call. Here came the cops, hell-bent for election. It was shoot or run. I didn't . . . Well, I just wasn't brought up to run. Luckily I didn't kill anyone either. The police shot all the windows out of the building before my cartridges gave out. Then I discovered what a white bunch Easterners really are. Every man I'd knocked down came into court the next morning and testified it was his own fault. I got off with a fine for disturbance. But the faculty called me onto the carpet and suspended me for six months. But I had a couple of pow-wows with prexy, explained the whole thing, and was permitted to go on. After that I hocked my gun. I've never worn one since."

"You mean — you sold your saddle?" Red asked in a tone of unbelief.

"I sold my saddle," answered Tobasco, interpreting the expression of the old West, which denoted the greatest disgrace that could come to a puncher, as being applicable also to his gun. "I haven't worn a forty-five for four years and I'm glad."

"You mean *lucky*," Chuckwallow cut in sourly. "Lucky you were at college instead of riding around this hell-crazy range."

"Lucky then," Tobasco rejoined. "But the fact remains just the same; if a fellow hasn't a gun, he can't use one. Naturally he relies on his fists or his brains. And you'll get farther with either in the long run." A hard note crept into his voice. "If I'd been toting an iron, I'd have killed two men today!"

Came a moment of silence; breathless, motionless silence. The remark was fired point blank at Chuckwallow. Now the men were certain the break had come. The foreman stood above Tobasco, eyeing him steadily. A faint drumming of hoofs suddenly drifted in on the night air. The youth got lazily to his feet. The tension broke. The punchers too sprang up.

"Reckon you was alluding to me in what you said about croaking two men today?" Chuckwallow blurted out angrily.

"Yes," Tobasco admitted. "I'd have killed you back at the ranch when that shot was fired, because I was mad and nervous when I caught sight of you —"

"But you didn't think I tried to plug you, did you?" A note of hope rang loud in Grayson's query.

The youth dropped a hand onto the old cowman's shoulder.

"I know you didn't fire that shot, Chuckwallow," he said earnestly. "For two reasons . . . first, it came from behind. When you shoot a man, it will be between the eyes, not the shoulder blades. Second, because I heard the jasper who fired that shot ride away. I followed him, he had two pals with him, but I lost them right in here somewhere."

Far from satisfied in their own minds that Grayson had not attempted to get revenge, the punchers heard the youth in astonishment. They could scarcely believe their eyes when Chuckwallow extended his hand.

"Shake," he said in an unsteady voice. "I'm for you, dude pants and all. I can see where you had a license to smoke me up if you'd of had a gun. Mebby the ideas you're preaching ain't so crazy after all. But who was the other fellow you'd of plugged?"

Tobasco gripped the extended hand eagerly.

"Soapy Stevens!" he replied.

Chuckwallow was silent for a moment listening to the hoofbeats, which were growing louder.

"Let me tell you something, son," he said soberly. "It don't matter what you think of toting an iron, if you twist tails with that hombre again you'd better be heeled to come a-shooting. He's bad . . . Worse than that, he's fanned a trigger with the best of them. He's going to pull a crooked play here before long that will make you forget your new-fangled notions. And get this . . . it ain't going to be no common lead slinger as settles Soapy Stevens' hash. You mark my words . . . it'll be you, Tobasco, because you're the only man who ever rode the Chimney Rock range that can beat Soapy Stevens to the draw. When that time comes, son, be sure you're got your forty-five, for there'll be no quarter!"

Tobasco heard him through ears in which blood that cried for violence had pounded incessantly since Peggy's confession back at the Horseshoe. The old foreman's words found echo in his heart. Whirling, he strode off a short distance, wondering if he was strong enough to stifle the longing for the old life beating so wildly within him. He could feel the eyes of the group upon him. He sensed the change that had come over them. Friendliness now was plain upon their rugged, homely faces. Gone in a flash was their reticence, their mistrust. He knew they were eager for him to accept the leadership — with smoking Colt and whining lead. His heart sank at thought of their accusing gaze when he refused.

His teeth clicked grimly. The light of resolute purpose shone in his eyes. He turned to rejoin them just as the sheriff, followed by Lonesome and the coroner, galloped up.

"What's going on here?" Kazen demanded, spurring his snorting horse as near as possible to the carcasses.

"Two Lazy JP steers butchered," Tobe answered, stepping forward. "Here are the hides."

"Who done it?"

Tobasco laughed.

"That's what you're going to figure out."

"Me?" Kazen exploded. "Do you mean to say a Pepper is going to turn a case of rustling and beef killing over for the law to handle?"

"That's exactly what I'm doing. There are several other things I'm going to turn over to you. First . . ." In spite of his valiant effort his voice broke. "I expect Lonesome has told you . . . Somebody — killed — Dad . . . Somebody took a shot at me near the ranch gate. I followed him and his two partners, lost them right in here. Now it's two critters butchered."

The officer swung down and stamped to his side. "Tobasco," he said, "there was a time when I was itching to send you to the pen. I can't understand what's come over you. If a few more of these hard-headed rannyhans would begin thinking your way, it would be a heap easier to keep law and order. I'm right sorry to hear about your paw . . . I'll do my damnedest to help you, son."

Chuckwallow ripped out an oath under his breath, kicked his horse in the ribs with such violence that it almost tore the bridle reins from his hand as it lunged away.

"What's the matter with you?" Kazen demanded sharply.

"Nothing!" the foreman spat disgustedly. "Only you two old women make me sick the way you're boosting the law that ain't done nothing for this country but fill up the jails with little gobblers and let the big rustlers run around loose." He swung into the saddle. The others secured their horses and followed suit. They were all mounted presently and headed back toward the Lazy JP.

"Joe," Tobe asked spurring alongside of the sheriff. "Who owns the Circle R?"

"You've got me," Kazen confessed. "I'd give my right leg to find out. Why?"

"Nothing." Tobasco rode along in silence for a moment. "But . . . Doesn't anyone know?"

"Not that I've ever seen or heard," was the sheriff's answer. "I'm working on it though . . . And when I find out, I reckon . . ." He stopped short. Always a man who kept his own council, he already had said too much.

"Did you know Jake Elliot was dead?" Tobe offered after a time in a guarded tone as they jogged along.

"Jake Elliot dead!" Kazen exclaimed blankly, reining in his horse. "Hell, no! Who said so?"

"I got it straight," Tobasco told him. "But keep it under your hat for awhile. I just wanted to tip you off, you understand?" The sheriff nodded. "He died two years ago — back East somewhere."

"The hell you say?" Kazen blurted out, roweling his pony ahead. "Old Jake Elliot dead. Danged if I can hardly believe it. Funny it never leaked out . . . But . . . It reminds me of something I almost forgot. Old Jake came to me about two years ago. Seemed like there was something on his mind; I tried to worm it out of him, but he would only say he reckoned he was going to die some time. He gave me a package of papers. Told me if anything ever happened, to turn them over to Peggy. Reckon it must be his will. But Peggy or nobody else has ever called for it."

"Probably no one knows you have them," Tobe answered thoughtfully. "But it can't be his will because he made one — left the ranch jointly to Peggy . . . and Stevens. It's funny —"

"The hell!" Kazen flashed in unbelief.

They skirted a dry wash, shortened the distance between them and the rest of the party.

"But say, Tobe," Kazen remarked after a time, "while we're hunting for this other, keep your eye peeled for a hombre with two fingers missing from his gun hand. He's 'Two Finger' Brown, one of the dangdest gun-toters and killers running loose." He could not see the sudden tensing of Tobasco's body. "Broke out of jail down in Colorado. Just got a circular today — there's a big reward for him. Not being in the man-hunting business, that probably don't interest you . . . But mebbyso he has drifted onto this hell-crazy range. You never can tell. They all seem to. The circular said he was a pal of another hombre . . . Can't just recall right off what his high-faluting monicker was . . . Oh, yes — 'Cimarron' George. This Cimarron fellow got out of the Southwest two or three years back, after he'd killed a couple of deputies and smoked up a town. They are bad hombres. The authorities down there kind of think they've teamed up somewheres again. They've both got a naked lady tattooed on their chests. They were in the navy together and deserted. Don't reckon the identifying marks will help any, for, considering the calibre of men they are, nobody would hanker after snaking their shirts off to see. But it's just possible they've come in here with all this flock of nesters. So keep your eye peeled."

"Joe!" Tobasco lowered his voice. "Two-Finger Brown killed Dad!"

"What?" Kazen ejaculated. "How do you know?"

"Just before Dad died he said something about 'two fingers missing.' I recall it particularly, because one of the three men I told Johnson to run out of town, when I had my fight with Stevens at the Goldbug, in Bigtrails, was minus two fingers on his right hand!"

"Huh!" Kazen grunted. "Reckon then we had better keep our eyes peeled sharp. You've started packing your gun again, haven't you?"

"No."

"Better strap her on, son. I'd like to pin a badge onto you and make you a deputy sheriff until we get this thing straightened out."

Tobasco gritted his teeth savagely on the passionate longing to return to the old life which had taken such powerful hold upon him. His heart leaped at the sheriff's words. Here was a chance to know the feel of a forty-five nestling against his hip; an opportunity to salve a rebellious conscience with the knowledge he was carrying it in the name of the law. A kaleidoscopic review flashed before his mind with dizzy speed ... A picture of his father ... Stevens ... Peggy!

This time it was even more difficult than before to stifle his wild desire.

"No, Joe," he answered firmly. "God knows I'm a gun-slinger by instinct ... I long to ... But with the killing of Dad, the shot at me — another I haven't told you about — I can't trust myself. I'm into things too deep already to be a deputy. If I'm forced to shoot, it will be for the Lazy JP, not the law. I'm going to get to the bottom of this mess in my own way. The man who murdered Dad knew about a lease taken out by the Horseshoe on our state section with the water-holes on it. The fellow who took a crack at me started for the Horseshoe, but changed his course. After I'd lost the trail of the three, I rode on to the ranch."

"What ranch?" asked Kazen.

"The Horseshoe."

"Did you take your gang along?"

"No."

"Have any gunplay?"

Tobasco hesitated. On the verge of telling the sheriff of his fight with Stevens, he decided to spare Peggy more unpleasantness and protect her as best he could.

"I didn't even have a gun," he replied evasively.

The officer shot him a piercing look. "Hell's bobcats!" he snorted. The outburst past, he fell to musing. "So old Jake is dead? With your paw and him both gone, I reckon now we can get a quick settlement to this range feud."

"We cannot!" Tobe's voice was metallic in its hardness. "They've leased that state section and cut us off from our water-holes. Joe, there hasn't been any trouble yet. The real hell has just begun on the Chimney Rock."

Kazen jerked his head sagely although the judicial wagging was lost in the darkness.

"There's hell enough without you tearing loose with your smoke-pole like you used to, Tobasco," he cautioned. "But you sure have got the old nerve even if you do wear dude pants and puttees." The youth jerked straight in his saddle and stared ahead to where Chuckwallow had pulled rein to give instructions to the two riders, returning with their bedrolls to guard the carcasses.

CHAPTER
TEN

The funeral of old Jackson Pepper was a simple affair, yet touched with a poignancy of which the rough-and-tumble old West seemed incapable. A few hymns in the rambling old living room of the Lazy JP ranch-house, jammed to overflowing with friends — Drab, red-eyed women in calico, traces of faded beauty still on their faces which showed the ineradicable stamp of the prairie that left them prematurely old and withered . . . Rough-mannered men, faces blackened and pitted by sun and wind, choking, plainly ill at ease in starched collars and poorly-fitting "store" clothes. Outside in the yard milled men in faded and patched denim; punchers in chaps, who for the moment had laid aside their spurs to lend quiet to their shambling movements.

The songs ended . . . A simple eulogy . . . The cortege moved to the hogback overlooking the ranch. There, with the afternoon sun blazing down upon the thirsty prairies, old Jackson Pepper was laid to his last rest, the rim-rock he loved so well his tombstone, the quavering wail of a coyote his requiem.

There were few tears, fewer regrets. Grim-faced men passed by for a final glimpse with only a tightening of jaws. There was no demonstration, it was the way of the old West.

After the simple rites, Tobasco saddled a horse and rode out from the ranch in search of solitude. His heart was filled to bursting with grief at his father's death, with the renewed avowals of old friendship that had touched him mightily. But still another thing preyed on his mind . . . A thing that hurt far deeper than he would even admit to himself. The oldest unwritten law of Rangeland had been violated — there had been no representative of the Horseshoe at the funeral. He choked back a surge of bitterness toward Peggy for the oversight. But then, he had looked and watched for Peggy herself in vain.

The days that passed found him plunging into work in a frantic effort to keep his mind occupied. Idleness set his brain to whirling. The loss of his father, the hatred that was consuming the once peaceful range, Peggy's absence, drove him to the point of madness. These things, together with a soul crying out for vengeance, kept him in a constant turmoil.

He went from one end of the big ranch-house to the other, cleaning out drawers, hunting every slip of paper, every receipt. These he piled on a growing heap on his father's untidy desk. Then, when he had collected everything, he fell to work; methodical work, checking, rechecking studying time-worn documents, maps, surveyor's plots, posting himself on the minutest detail of the Lazy JP. He paid no attention to the work outside. And, under the watchful eye of old

Chuckwallow, the men went quietly about their tasks, the routine scarcely interrupted save that no longer was fiery old Jackson Pepper about to curse them into action.

A week dragged thus, with the men catching only an occasional glimpse of Tobasco, when he dragged himself from his work and ate with them, or went to the bunkhouse of a night to lie on a bedroll smoking, staring silently up into space. They respected his silence; made no offer to draw him into conversation.

July burned itself to a crisp, leaving in its wake a scene of desolation; miles of bone-dry flats, seared and buff and withered. Came August's sun even more intense, almost insufferable, to lay like a scourge upon the blazing flats. But if Tobasco so much as noticed the heat he gave no sign. Doggedly he stuck to his work inside the ranch-house.

Then one day, near the middle of the month, he called old Chuckwallow from the horse corrals, where the crew was breaking out short strings for beef round-up. The old cowman came into the house mopping a grimy face with a bandana, oozing sweat in his brush-scarred leather chaps and awkward boots to find the youth cool and comfortable in puttees and moleskins. But if the comparison made any impression on Chuckwallow he would not mention it.

At a sign from Tobasco, the old cowman followed him across the room to a window. Ten riders had driven a herd of steers to the fence of the state section. They had ridden off a way and had engaged in a conference. Presently they rode back. Undoing their throw ropes, they hooked them over the wire and made a dally around their saddlehorns. The ponies lunged. The whining "ping-ping" of the parting barbed strands drifted in on the hot wind to the pair who stood watching in utter silence.

After the fence had been jerked down, the ten rode inside and took possession. Not until then did Chuckwallow move. He fell to cursing savagely. It was only with an effort Tobasco was able to restrain him.

"They can't tear down a fence like that!" Chuckwallow bawled. "We built it around that state section. It's ours."

"You're right, they can't," Tobasco conceded grimly. "But they did just the same. And now we have recourse to the courts. That's why I let them do it; why I called you in here to see them do it. I've been watching them work up to it for several days. Now, under the law, I can call for an appraisal of that fence. They'll buy it, don't worry. And they'll pay high for the destruction."

"Is that all you're going to do about it?" the foreman demanded incredulously.

"For now — yes," answered Tobe. "Keep your shirt on, Chuckwallow," he threw at Grayson, who slammed from the house and stormed toward the corrals still cursing loudly. "There are two sides to everything. By keeping our mouths shut we've got the law with us. And besides, what they've done so far has been too small to get us good and mad!"

Later, however, when Stevens himself rode up and threw a bunch of whitefaces in on the waterholes with the first herd, Tobasco hung onto his own furiously mounting temper with an effort.

He watched the Horseshoe foreman as he gave instructions to the ten men, then whirled and galloped away alone.

During the day, riders, mounted on spirited horses, rode up to the Lazy JP gate, watched from a distance, then loped on making no pretense of friendliness nor showing any intention of entering. Absorbed in the study of a large map, Tobasco paid them little heed.

"Chuckwallow," he said to his foreman, on one of the many trips to the house the cursing and fuming old cowhand suddenly had found necessary, "who do you suppose those riders are? And what are they doing?"

"I'd say they was milling around to see if we were going to lay down like a litter of kittens, without their eyes open, over that busted fence," Grayson snarled. "They're watching every move we make, sure as the devil."

Of the same opinion, Tobasco was yet reluctant to add to the excitement of the savage foreman, who already was bordering on eruption.

"Chuckwallow," he said, kicking a chair across to the cowman, who ignored it to pace about angrily chewing at the ends of his mustache, "how much water have we left?"

"Without rain, we've got enough over in Boxelder to get us by for about two weeks," Grayson rasped out sourly. "After that, I reckon the critters will give up the ghost, because there ain't another drop between here and the Horseshoe excepting what's to be had on that state section."

"Good!" Tobasco leaped up, lighted a cigaret and strode over to the window to gaze at the distant hills black in their mantle of Norway pine, slashed with green and gold of quaking aspens.

CHAPTER
ELEVEN

"Good?" Chuckwallow ejaculated hollowly, staring at Tobasco in unconcealed amazement. "I don't see anything very damned good about it."

Tobasco ignored the retort.

"I'm going to town for a couple of weeks," he said, turning presently. "You're in complete charge of the ranch, but with explicit orders not to have any trouble with the Horseshoe. By that I do not mean are you to take any insults or allow them to tear down another foot of fence. If any of their stock gets through into our pastures from the state section, drive them into the corrals and hold them as stray stuff and we'll notify the sheriff and Stock Association. While I'm gone I want you to round up every Lazy JP bunch that needs water and throw them into the home pasture."

"There ain't no water in there," Grayson snorted. "What do you want me to do, dip drinks out of the cistern and water them in a dipper twice a day?"

Tobasco smiled, a tired grim smile. "That will hardly be necessary. I want every hoof we own gathered by the time the holes dry up in Boxelder. Hold them until they are thirsty enough to go on the prod for water. Then I want you and the boys to tear down the division fence between this pasture and the state section!"

"Man alive!" Chuckwallow gasped. "You'd get your foot into it clean up to your knees doing anything like that."

"I've got a right to tear down any of my own fence, haven't I?" Tobe asked.

"Yep," Grayson admitted. "But you haven't got any more license than the Horseshoe has to bust the fence that the Lazy JP put around that state section years ago until after it's appraised and handled legally."

"That's where you're wrong, Chuckwallow," Tobasco put in quickly. He walked over to the litter of papers on the desk, which he had been studying. "We'll beat those fellows at their own game. Whether it was foresight on Dad's part or just bull-headed luck on ours, I don't know. But that division fence between the home pasture and those waterholes is fifteen feet off the state section . . . And it is on Lazy JP deeded land!"

"The devil you say!" Chuckwallow exploded. But a worried uncertain look quickly chased the gleam of pleasure from his eyes. "But there aren't men enough on the Chimney Rock range to hold thirsty cows from those water-holes without a division fence."

Tobasco shrugged significantly.

"There's no law to stop stampedes," he observed. "But there is one to make an outfit fence its land if it expects to keep other cattle out."

A great light began to dawn on Grayson. "God-a'mighty!" he blurted out. "Are —"

"Nothing can stop the Lazy JP critters when they get a scent of that water," Tobe cut in to grin. "Have your horses handy. Make a good bluff at turning them back . . . But be damned sure you don't do it! After they're filled up, take your time and throw the herd into the home pasture again to graze. After the first run they'll go onto the state section for water of their own accord when they get thirsty enough. Keep on making a show of trying to stop them . . . Only be damned sure you let them go. But for the Lord's sake don't let them get mixed with the Horseshoe stuff in there if you can possibly avoid it. By the time Stevens gets a division fence rebuilt I'll . . . Well, I'll be back."

"I'll try and stop 'em awright!" Chuckwallow nodded and winked knowingly.

"No fighting though, unless it's forced on you," Tobasco warned. Knowing the foreman understood and could be depended upon to follow his instructions without a hitch, he changed the subject abruptly.

"Do you know where the water-holes lay on the Horseshoe? It's been so long since I've had occasion to think of it I —"

"They use cistern water for the house. Then there's a big spring just off old Jake's original homestead. You recklect that spring came in years ago when they were drilling for water. Artesian flow. Old Jake was sure sore because it wasn't on his original section." He paused to eye the youth sharply. "Say!" he demanded in a hushed tone. "What the hell are you figurin'?"

"Never mind." Tobasco smiled enigmatically. "But you've got the right hunch. There will be a surveying

92

gang up here tomorrow. Don't pay any attention to them. They'll know exactly what to do. I'm going to have a re-run of every line on the Chimney Rock range. Of course, if they need help, that's what you're here for. When I come back I'll have another crew of men with me."

The foreman's eyes bulged. " 'Lowin' to clean house and give us fellows the go by?"

"Not on your life," Tobasco assured him. "You tried to quit and I wouldn't let you. No matter what you boys think of me and my dude pants, I wouldn't fire you if it was the last thing I did on earth. The Lazy JP is your home as long as you will stay. I'm going to run two gangs . . . You're going to be the foreman of them both."

"Say, Tobasco," Chuckwallow mumbled, twirling his hat awkwardly, and spinning his spur rowel on the rug, "I reckon I've — Oh, hell!" he blurted out. "You'll find things going along here, when you come back just like they are now. We'll do our damnedest to stop the stampede — just like you said — and I'll give you my word that unless those Horseshoe wallopers ride right up to the house and poke the muzzles of their guns in our faces, we won't open our yawps." He swung on his heel and strode out of the house. A short time later, Tobasco saw him in earnest conversation with the men who were grouped about, eagerly asking questions.

The youth returned to the litter of papers and dropped into a chair before the desk. A new tally he had compiled with infinite care from the mass of records showed four thousand head of Lazy JP cattle ranging the region. A large plot of the various holdings in the Chimney Rock area, with the sections of each of the outfits marked and a notation explaining the manner of acquiring the lease or patent, held his eye for a moment. And the open bank book beside him showed a balance of twenty thousand dollars, which his father had deposited after the spring shipping. Little enough, he concluded, to carry out the project he had in mind. Arising he paced about thoughtfully for a time, then, arranging the papers in a brief case, he too left the house and went to the corrals.

He saddled his horse in silence. The punchers went about their work moodily, making no offer to help him. While their mistrust had vanished, they avoided him, no longer because of his riding breeches and puttees, but because they were utterly ashamed of the way they had acted, and were reluctant to admit that they themselves had disrupted the old camaradery which they were eager to resume, had they but known how. Far different from other days when one or more of them would have ridden a piece with him. Tobasco mounted, and with only a brief word, headed for town.

For the first few miles of the thirty to Bigtrails he rode slowly, sunk in thought. He scarcely heeded the stretches of barren plain, the grasses seared and brown and rustling in the scorching sun; the prairie dogs that chirped defiance from the mounds on every side. Where before it would have sent him in wild pursuit, he now looked with unseeing eyes at the coyote which slunk from a dry wash, crossed the road, and stopped a scant hundred yards away to sit on its haunches and watch him. The hills, wrapped in their mantle of August haze, at times seemed almost upon him in the shimmering heat, then, again, so far distant they were but a smoke blue etching against the blazing sky.

He forged ahead, blind to the scenes around him. Suddenly he roweled his pony and urged it into a gallop. The burst of speed, the whipping of the sagespiced air in his face, momentarily relieved the tension of his mind which was haunted by the face of Peggy Elliot as he last had seen her, pleading with him to take her away, stark terror in her eyes at thought of the man she had wed.

It was after dark when he reached Bigtrails.

Then his mount was sidling nervously down the dimly-lighted street of the village, between rows of horses — flint-eyed broncos, lining the hitch rails, that shied and snorted as he rode past. From beyond the light came the squeal of other broncs, fighting savagely.

Riding to the livery barn, he crowded his mount beneath the lantern at the door, gave brief instructions for its care and strode back into the street.

Punchers jostled him; rough unshaven punchers, evil-faced, beady-eyed. Strangers all. Loud-voiced painted women ogled him. From the open doors of a honky-tonk came the banging of a piano, the scrape of a fiddle. Maudlin bass and coyote falsetto rose in ear-splitting discord. The dusk was eerie with shouts and screams. Even the cool breeze that now whipped in from the prairies, to sift sand against the false fronts of the straggling buildings, lent a mournful wail to the uproar.

The first saloon he passed was overflowing with cowboys, wild and untamed as the broncs that filled the street. A place new to him, that saloon. And the inmates . . . Not a familiar face. He went on, presently to pause outside the Goldbug. Here too was a bedlam of shouts, curses and ribald song. He pushed through the swinging doors. Punchers were prowling about, mopping sweat-beaded brows with gaudy kerchiefs. Punchers were hunched over poker tables. Punchers were slumped against the long pine bar with knees of tallow. The air reeked with the odor of sweaty leather and stale beer. Bigtrails, Tobasco thought grimly, was living up to her reputation.

Johnson, the bartender, spotted him and came up alongside quickly, full of sympathy at his father's death.

"I know how you feel about it, old-timer," Tobasco said, gripping the outstretched hand warmly. "You're one of the few left in these parts, I guess, who make me feel that I belong. But I'm playing a hunch, pardner. Keep your eye peeled for a hombre with two fingers missing from his gun-hand. He's the killer —"

The bartender did not wait for him to finish. He pointed to a big placard hanging in the center of the mirror along the back bar. It was a reward notice for Two-Finger Brown. Beneath in large letters had been printed: — "This jasper killed Jackson Pepper. The Goldbug will pay $500 in cash, in addition to the above reward, to any man who snakes this hombre in — feet first."

The eyes of the youth went dry, smarting. Here was friendship. Yet, well meant as it was, it would only serve to put the assassin, if he was still in the country, on his guard.

"What became of all those homesteaders you said were in town hunting locations?" Tobasco asked huskily when he was certain of his voice.

"There's six of the poor devils yonder leaning against the wall." The bartender jerked a thumb toward the opposite side of the saloon. "Why?"

"Oh, nothing." Tobasco drummed the bar thoughtfully for a moment. Then he dashed off a drink Johnson had placed before him and sauntered over to where the strangers were watching a poker game.

"Have something to drink, fellows?" he invited.

Surprised at the amiable greeting, after the many rebuffs they had encountered in the country where the stigma of being a nester never dies, they trailed silently behind Tobasco back to the bar. There, with a bottle passing among them, he held them in earnest conversation for a considerable time. When finally they reached some agreement, they went with him from the saloon to the hotel, where, over the map he took from his brief case, they sat talking far into the night. Tobasco left them to return after a time with Sheriff Joe Kazen. Dawn was lifting along the rim of the prairies in a fling of vivid color when the conference ended and Kazen went back to the jail, the others to bed.

CHAPTER
TWELVE

Back at the Lazy JP, a relentless August sun had upset Chuckwallow's calculations. It beat down on the flats until they were griddle-hot, radiating heat like the top of a stove, setting the prairies to dancing like a mirage. It burned the grasses on the stem, leaving them drab and buff and seared. It turned the chain of tepid, greenish waterholes dotting the gumbo bed of Boxelder to mud-holes over night. And to make matters worse, scarcely a week had elapsed after Tobasco's departure, when Lonesome, riding in one noon with a small bunch of gaunt-flanked, thirsty pickups he had gathered in the brakes, reported not a drop of water left for the panting cattle.

In spite of his elation at the feasibility of Tobasco's plan, which he had had ample time to ponder and over which he gloated in secret, Lonesome's announcement sent a chill to old Chuckwallow's heart. Too well he knew what the grave-faced cowboy's discovery meant. Many times before he had seen prowling herds on the dusty wastes, bellowing piteously, pawing at sun-cracked mud-holes, only to drop in their tracks from thirst and exhaustion. He had watched the frantic brutes pitch about in the creek beds, trying to puddle

98

themselves a few putrid drops, only to be mired down, too weak to rise. There were others that drifted on and on in search of water, finally to go down in the arid dry washes, or to pace frantically the length of a drift fence barring their advance until they, too, finally went down. The following spring a pile of bleached bones was mute evidence of their hopeless struggle. It was the great tragedy of Cowland, that constant driving need for water.

Chuckwallow's gaze roamed to the sky. It glittered like a sheet of tin, its vast glaring expanse unbroken by a single cloud. Thirty years on the range had given him an uncanny knowledge of the weather. Without a drop of moisture to relieve the situation, the stifling heat would continue until fall. Then broiling summer would give way, almost in a day, to winter — frigid, death-dealing winter that would lash the open range with arctic fury. What cattle could survive the drought would go into the blizzards with scant hope of pulling through.

Save for a few scattered head, every hoof bearing a Lazy JP brand had been thrown inside the pasture fence. Jammed hip to hip, the bawling animals were milling about restlessly, tormented by thirst.

Basing his hope on the reckoning he had given Tobasco that there was enough water for still another week, Chuckwallow himself had thought little of this crisis. In fact, he had spent the entire time with the surveying party which, as Tobasco had told him, would come out from town.

Now that the emergency had come, he moved swiftly to meet it. Calling the punchers to the ranch-house, he gave them their first intimation of Tobasco's plan.

"Lonesome says the water-holes have dried up," he announced grimly. "That being the case, I want every mother's son of you to roll out before daylight. We're going to give up punching cows for a spell and go to yanking down fence."

"That'll be a fine job this kind of weather," Red groaned, lifting his Stetson to push back a damp mop of fiery hair from a sweat-beaded brow. "What fence are you aiming to tear down — if it ain't a secret?"

"That division fence on the state section." Chuckwallow fairly bristled with importance.

"But that'll let Lazy JP critters into the waterholes," Cactus argued judiciously.

"Well?" Old Chuckwallow failed in an attempt to imitate Tobasco's careless shrug. "There ain't no law to stop stampedes. We'll try our best to stop 'em." He winked broadly at the men. "But water's what we want. And water's what we've got to have. After they've filled up, we'll turn 'em back to this pasture."

Thunderstruck at the daring of the scheme, but reluctant to ask questions that might bring about a cancellation of the order, which was decidedly to their liking, and which they thought Chuckwallow had issued of his own initiative, the punchers quickly left the house.

During the afternoon their tuneless songs, the ribald jibes they hurled in answer to the orders the instrument

100

men of the surveying party were shouting to their chainmen, reflected their lightened spirits.

Before sun-up they were jerking the wire from the division fence, uprooting the posts with throwropes dallied around their saddlehorns, and howling at the cattle which were grouped about staring at them inquisitively.

Chuckwallow, his faded eyes glittering, sat a rangy sorrel in readiness to swing into the head of the herd the moment the fence was down. He kept a weather eye cocked on the state section, at the far end of which he could see the ten punchers Stevens had left, driving their herd back from the waterholes to graze.

Suddenly the wind shifted. The thirsty cattle caught the scent of water. Somewhere a steer threw up its head, let forth a throaty bawl, rolled its tail and started away at a lumbering trot. That bellow was quickly caught up, rose to a crescendo tumult in a thousand different tones. The herd was gone in a sea of rocking rumps and clashing horns.

"For Gosh sake, stop 'em! Stop 'em! Heel-fly 'em!" laughed Chuckwallow, motioning frantically to the punchers, who had scattered from the pounding hoofs and thrown themselves into the saddles.

"Don't let the herds get mixed!" he warned as he galloped back among the punchers, who were barking and howling at the edges of the surging torrent. "If anything like that happens we'll sure see more trouble than we ever believed there was on earth."

By now the herd, driven frantic by the scent of water, had bunched and was thundering along in stampede, like an angry, foaming river at flood stage, sweeping everything before it, crushing down all in its path that dared defy its devastating advance. The incessant rumble of hoofs, the clicking of horns, the hoarse bawls combined to produce a bedlam, made more horrible by the sickening heat and the clouds of choking dust that rolled skyward to settle back in dirty-gray waves. It was a maddened, blinded mass, tearing across the flats; slavering brutes smashing through ravines, hurtling clumps of brush, dodging impossible jumps only to be jostled aside by their oncoming mates.

Suddenly a raw-boned steer at the head of the bunch sighted the herd of Horseshoes. A bawl of defiance rolled across the section. The challenge was caught up along the whole line. The pasture echoed with the tumult.

"Hold 'em! Hold 'em!" yelled Chuckwallow, now thoroughly aroused and roweling back and forth in front of the herd, which suddenly had stopped, to stand, heads up, tails straight out like rudders. Then, as if to add to their difficulties, the other herd, led by a grumbling bull, which paused occasionally to paw a cloud of dust over his back, started forward.

The pause was brief, the scent of water too impelling. With low bawls of anticipation, the thirsty Lazy JP bunch was gone again to the thunder of pounding hoofs.

"Cut them Horseshoe critters back!" roared Chuckwallow, now fighting in earnest at the edge of the rushing herd to hold it on a straight course toward the springs. "Lonesome . . . Take all the men and meet that

102

Horseshoe bunch! Stand guard on 'em . . . Ours'll run until they hit them holes. But hold them others back or there'll be hell to pay proper."

He raced on at a long, swinging gallop beside the stampede. He risked a glance. Before his men were able to check the precipitate charge of the Horseshoe bunch, the leaders had veered sharply, dodged past them. Led by the great, white-faced bull, they too were thundering toward the waterholes.

"Well," Grayson observed aloud as he pulled his horse to a walk. "We've done our best. If they hadn't wanted the herds mixed they should have stayed off our ground."

The Lazy JP cattle were the first to reach the springs. They plunged ankle deep into the cooling water, waded into the middle of the pools, scooping the water into their parched mouths and letting it trickle over their reeking jowls. They had downed but a few feverish gulps when the sniffing, wildeyed Horseshoe herd was upon them. In an instant, the two bunches were hopelessly mixed.

Pandemonium broke loose. Brutes went down in struggling heaps. Hoarse bellows of pain drowned out the shouts, curses and the roar of forty-fives. Back and forth swayed the two lines, horns locked, neither gaining, neither giving ground. The water was whipped to a muddy slime.

"What in hell do you think you're doing?" thundered a bearded cowhand with an ugly lantern jaw, galloping up alongside of Chuckwallow. "What business you got bringing them Lazy JP critters in here, anyhow?"

Grayson jerked rein, grinned, swept the man, a stranger, from head to toe in a single insolent glance. The moment was poignant; the setting ideal for the showdown the old cowman secretly had hoped for weeks would come. He shifted sidewise in his saddle to throw his weight in one stirrup. Then with maddening deliberation he found tobacco and papers in his shirt pocket and coolly twisted a cigaret.

"Didn't you ever see a stampede before?" he asked mockingly, when he had cupped a match to the quirly, carefully extinguished it and flipped it away. "Or did you think maybe we was hunting buffalo?"

"Don't get lippy!" the fellow snarled. "You ain't got no business in here. You'd better get them critters of yours gathered up and get out of here before there's trouble."

"I know we ain't got no business in here," Chuckwallow threw back hotly. "But cows ain't partic'lar whose ground they stampede onto if you've ever noticed. You seen us doing our best to stop 'em, didn't you? Ever have any luck stopping a stampede, jasper?"

"You yanked down that division fence just so they would come in here," the stranger charged. "We've been watching you ever since you rode out there. And I'm telling you, you'd better get that fence strung back up or you'll catch merry hell for yanking it down."

"It's our fence." Chuckwallow took a deep drag on his cigaret and expelled the smoke through his nostrils. "We've tore it down, and we'll put it up — when we get damned good and ready. Wasn't our fault these pesky critters stampeded!"

"The hell it ain't your fault," the stranger ground between his teeth. "And it ain't your fence. It's on this state section and —"

"It is ours!" An ugly scowl deepened the wrinkles of Chuckwallow's weather-pitted face. "Our boss says so. He's a lawyer. And don't think for a minute he don't know what he's talking about. And it ain't for the likes of you, nor nobody else, to call him a liar!" He paused to give the cowboy a chance to take up the challenge. But he did not.

"We didn't aim to mix the herds." Chuckwallow toned down his incisive voice. "We was only trying to stop the stampede. But I reckon now they're mixed from hell to breakfast in spite of all we did or can do. If you wallopers will go over yonder somewhere and set down, my boys will show you how to untangle cows so fast it'll make your head swim."

"You ain't going to water in them holes!" the puncher flared. "Here, fellers!" he shouted to his nine men, all strangers, who had come up behind him to sit their horses tense, rigid. "Get into that bunch of critters and kill everything toting a Lazy JP mark. We'll show this old bullbat whether he can pull down fences and let his stuff in here to mix it with ours."

"Yeah!" Chuckwallow bawled. "Just try something like that. Just look like you even want to try something like that. For every critter you drop we'll plug one of your men and two head of your cows for good measure. Hop to it! Kill 'em if you feel your luckiest!"

In spite of the reckless impulse he voiced he was still struggling with himself to keep inviolate the confidence Tobasco had reposed in him. Plainly disappointed that they did not take up his challenge, still he fought half-heartedly to control the fury that was boiling up within him, but which yet was steadying his gun-arm.

"Ain't you going to do it?" he snorted in a tone that was little short of an invitation to the strangers to start the slaughter. "We're waiting."

When the cowboys made no move, he risked a glance at his own men, who, having failed in their efforts to stem the onrush of the Horseshoe animals, had taken heed of the danger signal in the old foreman's tones and ridden up behind him. They sat their horses easily, unperturbed. It was evident by their unconcealed grins that the outlook for an open break was to their liking also.

"We're willing to untangle them herds." Chuckwallow whirled back to the first stranger. "We ain't asking you to help a lick. It was our fault they mixed — but we couldn't keep them from stampeding." A smug satisfied expression settled on his face. From the corner of his eye he could see that the Lazy JP critters, having slaked their thirst, were straggling from the water-holes to sniff and horn at the Horseshoe animals, which were backing off and circling gingerly.

"You didn't have no business tearing down that fence and giving your cows a chance to get away from you!" the Horseshoe man grated. His forty-five seemed, to leap to the rim of its holster, spit flame. But swift as was his movement the one Chuckwallow made was even

106

swifter. Like a flash of light he drew, fired, and resumed his calm dragging on the cigaret, the blue smoke from his hot-barrelled forty-five blending with cigaret smoke to wreath about his head. The man reeled drunkenly in his saddle. His horse lunged, whirled about and bolted. Clutching the horn he succeeded in maintaining his seat.

A second of breathless silence, tense deadly silence broken only by the pounding of the terrified horse's hoofs and the sniffs of milling cattle. Then one of the strangers ripped out a savage oath and went for his Colt. His companions, waiting for someone to make a break, drew and blazed away. With bloodcurdling yells, the Lazy JP men cut loose. The ponies, crazed by the cracking guns, reared and plunged in frantic attempts to flee from the mêlée. Bullets "pinged" through the cloud of dust kicked up by the dancing hoofs; went whining away across the flats. A bellow of agony rose above the hoarse shouts and curses. One of the stranger's horses went down to stretch out and beat the ground with its head. Its rider managed to throw himself clear, crawl through the brush and drop from sight over the rim of a dry wash.

The battle ceased as suddenly as it had begun. Roweling his snorting mount into the choking mass, Chuckwallow leaped down. At his feet stretched a lifeless pony; another was struggling to rise. But the men had disappeared into a deep coulée within a stone's throw.

"Here, Lonesome!" Grayson bellowed. "You and Cactus keep your eye peeled for them hombres. Don't reckon they'll start nothing more with us, but you can't tell which way a snake will strike. Meanwhile me and the rest of the boys will sift our critters out of this mess." He paused, scratching his head thoughtfully. "Wouldn't it beat you?" he snorted. "Been on this hell-crazy range forty years . . . Thought I knowed every cowhand . . . First gang I get tangled up with, I don't know a blamed galoot. Cateye!" he added as an after-thought. "You ride for the sheriff. Not for me It's all a pack of damn foolishness . . . But I reckon that's what Tobasco would want us to do." He stared hard at his men. "The kid's gone plumb loco on letting the law take its course. I'm asking you — did we start this fight or not?"

"Nope," came the unanimous reply.

"You handled her like a real general and in the name of the law!" Lonesome added solemnly, stifling a grin with the back of a grimy hand.

"Wish I knowed more law," Chuckwallow pondered. "As long as they started it, and we give 'em the worst of it, do you 'spose we'd be loping into the pen if we rode down in that draw and smoked 'em out?"

Before anyone could reply, a rifle cracked from the ravine. The bullet threw up a puff of dust at Grayson's feet. He dropped to his knees. The punchers followed suit.

"Get under cover," Chuckwallow shouted, dragging a carbine from beneath his stirrup leather and pumping a shell into the barrel. "Get them hosses of ours down in that next gully, Red. Now we can't move our critters. I'm damned certain there ain't no statute, as Tobasco

108

says, that will make us untangle them herds under gunfire . . . As long as them hombres ain't killing no cows, I reckon we ain't got no kick a-coming. Our cows have got plenty of water and good feed." He stretched out comfortably in a dry wash as another bullet whined harmlessly overhead. "Let's snooze, fellows. This is a dang sight softer than I figured."

CHAPTER
THIRTEEN

But if things were in a state of wild disorder and uncertainty at the Lazy JP, they were far from running smoothly at the neighboring Horseshoe.

Following his cowardly attack upon Tobasco, and the subsequent fight — of which he recalled little or nothing, he had been taken so completely by surprise — Soapy Stevens groped back to his senses on a bedroll in the bunkhouse. His first conscious thought was of loud snoring about him. The knowledge that the Horseshoe punchers could sleep without caring whether or not he did, angered him beyond reason. A splitting headache, a badly discolored eye, swollen shut and shot with throbbing pain, fanned that anger into rage. Savage curses sprang to his parched lips. But the violent outburst wracked a lumpy jaw.

He lay for a considerable time peering out of one eye into the darkness, his fury mounting with each passing minute. He tried desperately to collect his scattered wits and recall what had happened. When, presently he was able to snatch hazy mind pictures of the affair, the recollection brought him to his feet to reel outside, prey to a consuming rage.

Daylight found him in an ugly mood; venting his spleen upon the hapless men, cursing them for the most trivial things, crowding them at top speed in the blistering heat. The blazing sun, that wilted man and beast, the incessant persecution that rubbed raw nerves rawer, drove them almost to the point of rebellion. But fear, deadly fear of Stevens held them silent, tempered their furtive glances with meekness.

Up at the big ranch-house there was no sign of life, for Peggy had remained inside. Several times Stevens was on the point of calling her to account, but no opportunity presenting itself, he bided his time.

For several days he prowled about, cursing and fuming. Then one afternoon his smouldering fury got the best of him. Leaving his work abruptly, he strode to the house, resolved to force a showdown; to demand . . .

He was met at the door by the cook, armed with a long butcher knife and informed in no uncertain terms that Peggy was not to be disturbed.

Soapy's contemptuous gaze flashed up along the stubby bowed legs, the ample paunch, heaving with excitement, finally to come to rest on the cook's face, chubby, round as a boy's.

"Who the hell do you . . ." Soapy sputtered furiously. "You damned dough-slinger — get the hell out of the way!"

He took a step forward. The keen-edged knife came up menacingly. With the inherent dread every gun-toter possesses of a knife, Stevens recoiled. Something in the cook's faded, watery blue eyes warned him to tread easy, either that or shoot, for Soapy knew cooks — especially round-up cooks, as the old fellow once had been. They are toy gods of their own domain, cock-of-the-roost, fearless, domineering, deadly in action; and this fellow, whom old Jake Elliot had planted in the kitchen of the Horseshoe ranch-house after his warped legs had become too stiff to scale a bedwagon, was no exception to the rule.

"I've been with this spread for twenty years," the cook snarled back, thumbing the blade, "and I ain't never took no yawp from no damned bowlegged bullbat of a cow rannyhan yet. An' I'm too danged old to begin taking orders from your kind now. You try to go in there to devil the life out of Miss Peggy and I'll carve you into hunks and use you for coyote bait."

Stevens roared with laughter. Yet it was hoarse, nervous. He braced himself, spread-legged. His thumb slid down to hook itself in his cartridge belt near the butt of his forty-five.

"You pack your warbag and hit the grit," he rasped out. "I'm running this Horseshoe spread. And I won't have no kittle-paunched dough-mixer telling me what I can do and what I can't."

"He'll do nothing of the kind!"

Attracted by the loud voices, Peggy herself had come to investigate. She stood just inside the door, her black eyes snapping, her fists clenched until the kunckles were bloodless with the pressure.

"Go on back to the kitchen, John," she told the cook quietly. "And you . . ." She faced Soapy furiously. "You get away from this house and stay away."

A slow pale shade blotted the tan from Stevens' cheeks. Involuntarily his hand fell to his gun. He caught the slip quickly, jerked back to rehook his thumbs in his cartridge belt.

"I was going to give you a chance to talk things over," he sneered. "But now — I caught that damned Pepper making love to you. I —"

"Stop right there!" she flashed. "Mr. Pepper — did not understand. But if he had . . ." She stopped, suddenly conscious of the flame in her cheeks.

"It wouldn't have made no difference, I expect you was going to say." Soapy completed the sentence in the words she had checked on her lips. "What you blushing about? You don't want to forget I'm your husband. And I've got grounds for a divorce right now if I want it."

A sudden shudder racked her. She moved back away from him.

"You — you — beast!" she cried. "If you ever come into this house again I'll — I'll — kill — you!" She slammed the door in his face. He heard the key turn in the lock.

"You little hell cat!" he spat, glaring at the weather-stained panels. "Two can play at that game. I'll get even, don't worry. I'm going to plug that sweetheart of yours, if it's the last thing I do. I haven't forgot he cracked me in the jaw when I wasn't looking!" He spun about and stamped from the porch.

From behind the curtains of the window Peggy watched him. He had taken but a few steps, when a puncher came running up. She saw Stevens stop, whirl and sweep the Bigtrails road in the direction the excited cowboy was pointing. She followed his gaze.

The strangest caravan the Chimney Rock range had ever witnessed was pulling up at the Horseshoe gate!

In the lead rode six horsemen. Following were eight four-horse teams heaving in taut traces of wagons loaded to the standards with lumber and building material. Back of these sputtered a couple of dilapidated automobiles. Then two caterpillar tractors.

Consumed with curiosity, Peggy ventured outside, her anger momentarily forgotten at the strange sight.

"What . . . What is it?" she asked timidly of Stevens, who had stood motionless just off the steps.

He turned on her eyes in which the fire of passion still smouldered.

"Looks like your friend, Mr. Pepper, coming to visit you again!" he rasped out, leaving abruptly and striding down the road to meet the group.

She went chalk-white under his brutal words. Tears of anger sprang to her eyes. She dashed them away furiously. Then, of a sudden, her wilted figure jerked straight. She felt the blood rush to her face. The man astride the lead horse was Tobasco. And beside him rode Sheriff Joe Kazen!

Stevens, his legs spraddled wide, his hand on his gun, had stopped the caravan a short distance below the house.

Taking a grip on her quivering nerves, Peggy ran swiftly toward the group. She caught Tobasco's eye. Again the burning flood swept into her cheeks and temples. She could feel her heart thumping wildly. But

114

save for a smile that stirred her to the depths of her soul, Tobasco paid less heed to her than to the others.

"Where do you think you're going with that outfit?" Soapy demanded belligerently.

"Homesteading." Tobasco's quiet careless reply, in which lurked a sinister note of challenge, caused Peggy's heart to miss a beat. Her fearful gaze noted that the youth was unarmed. She waited with bated breath for Stevens' next words.

"There ain't no homesteads around here," he exploded. "You'd better swing back while you're all together. And we ain't turned our pastures into roads for damned nesters yet, by a hell of a ways. Rain-beaters are just as popular around here as the hoof-and-mouth disease. There's no land open to entry."

"That's where you are wrong, Stevens," Tobasco shot back with a cool and tantalizing smile. "As usual." He shifted sidewise in his saddle, his gaze flashing over the old familiar ranch — a miniature city of sod-roofed cottonwood log buildings and corrals, sharp-etched in the blasting sun. "I'll admit there is nothing open for entry now . . . Because my six partners and I have filed on every available acre of it. As for crossing your land . . . That's why I brought — meet Joe Kazen, the sheriff, Stevens — Joe came along to supervise the tearing down of your fences so we won't have to have any trouble on that score."

He motioned to the teamsters. They clucked to the horses, which strained forward in the traces. Peggy stifled the scream that rose to her lips as Soapy's gun

115

started from its holster. But Joe Kazen rose to the occasion. His blue-nosed Colt leaped from its holster, jerked up.

"Stash it!" he warned Stevens. "This outfit is going across the Horseshoe, according to law and the order of the court. If you didn't have your illegal fence strung all over hell's half acre it wouldn't be necessary to cross your pastures. But the law gives every one of these men a right to an outlet to a highway. And the walloper who tries to stop them is under arrest. I ain't so sure I won't take you anyway . . . For making that false break toward your gun just now."

"There's no land under our fence anybody can homestead," Soapy thundered, jerking his hand away from his Colt which had frozen on the rim of its holster. "Why should they cross here? I tell you, I won't have that Lazy JP — jasper on the place. I've got plenty against him now."

Peggy's hand flew to her heart. She felt dizzy, nauseated at what she expected Stevens to say.

"We've got just plenty to settle," he bawled on. "Someday Pepper, I'm going to get even with you for prowling around here with my —"

Tobasco threw himself from his saddle.

"Finish that and I'll choke the life out of you if I hang for it," he shot out.

CHAPTER
FOURTEEN

For a third time the two faced each other in white-hot anger, each sizing the other up in swift, piercing glances; each striving to see behind the mask-like faces and read the other's mind. As before they both read courage, reckless courage bred of wild and desperate encounters; the utter fearlessness of men who had looked death in the face without the flicker of an eyelash.

In spite of Tobasco's sudden movement, Stevens did not give an inch; his only move a barely perceptible start of whipcord muscles suddenly gone taut. Something of a smile quirked his lips, insolent, challenging. The glance he dared at Kazen's forty-five was livid with contempt.

In spite of the thrill that had surged through her at Tobasco's quick defense, a sickening helpless impotence took violent hold on Peggy. Stark terror choked a cry in her throat, held her speechless, powerless to move.

The men sat their wagons immobile as stone. The Horseshoe punchers who had quit their work to join the group, involuntarily jerked back to safety, leaving open a lane between them. Cowland has a way of sensing swift tragedy.

The silence deepened until it was almost tangible. Kazen cleared his throat huskily, shifted his weight to one stirrup. Then suddenly, the blazing sun made Stevens aware of its intensity. He shook off beads of sweat that had popped out on his brow. One of the lead horses threw up its head, nickered. The tension snapped.

As quickly as it had flared up, Tobasco's anger was under control. The trace of a smile moved the corners of his own braced lips; the smile of a man who knows no fear.

"Someday you and I are going to mix, Stevens," he said with a coolness that was maddening. "And when we do, only one of us is going to ride away. As far as I am concerned, that time can't come any too quickly. You've shot off your head — now let me talk awhile. Where's Jake Elliot?"

Stevens' face was mask-like in its calm. Tobe understood the look he shot at the girl, and the something in her eyes that told him she had revealed the secret. Soapy evaded the snare cunningly.

"Died in the East two years ago," he answered in a tone as easy as Tobasco's own. "Why?" He noted that the news was no surprise. "You already knew it. It ain't no secret that I know of."

"Who leased that state section down at the Lazy JP?" was the next question Tobe fired point blank.

"The Horseshoe!" Stevens shot back the answer without batting an eye.

Peggy started violently.

"You never told me anything about it," she flashed.

"Haven't had time," Soapy retorted. "Tried to tell you when you —" She understood and was thankful he did not blurt out that she had slammed the door in his face.

"Is that your idea of fairness, leasing every drop of water we have on the place?" Tobe demanded.

"Ain't nothing to me whether you've got water or not," Soapy retorted callously. "I'm looking out for Horseshoe critters. We've only got a little left. The spring yonder —"

"That's what I'm leading up to," Tobe interrupted in a tone that carried a sinister note. "You'd feel all right about somebody getting hold of all your water the same way as you got ours, would you?"

Stevens tried to fathom the meaning hidden behind the query but failed.

"Not by a damned sight!" he snapped.

"Then you'll admit leasing that state section was as much spite work as anything else?" Tobe demanded.

Soapy's lips curled in a sneer. But he made no answer.

"Do you think it's necessary for your men to destroy fences to get possession . . . of property you have leased legally?"

"Our men will not destroy fences to get possession of anything," Peggy put in, the light of sudden resolution replacing fear in her eyes.

"They won't?" Tobe turned to her. "What if I told you they already had?"

The color left her face. His gaze darted back to Stevens.

"When?" Soapy demanded. "I never heard about it. I threwed the first bunch of Horseshoe stuff in there myself. There wasn't nothing said about tearing down no fences."

Tobasco knew the fellow was lying. Yet out of consideration for the girl, he did not pin him down. He was on the point of laying all the trouble, including the murder of his father and the mysterious shot in the moonlight to Stevens. But cold reason stayed the accusations that sprang to his lips. Stevens' presence at the Horseshoe ranch-house the night of the fight was positive proof that the foreman could not have been one of the three who had attempted to shoot him.

For the first time it came to his mind that Stevens had not put in an appearance until after he had been with Peggy for some time. But even with that he had no evidence — only a suspicion far too vague and senseless for an open charge. Nor had his father offered positive proof his slayer was a Horseshoe man. The exact words of the dying man were seared into his memory:

"'They was old Jake's men sure, or they wouldn't have knowed it.'"

Recognizing nothing was to be gained by the accusations and needlessly adding to the worry of the girl, he turned the subject.

"There's a lot of rustling going on right now," he remarked pointedly. "Had you noticed it, Stevens?"

"We've lost some." The foreman's answer was guarded, crafty.

"Any of your stuff been slaughtered?"

"That's none of your damned business!" Stevens blazed. "Say, what do you think this is anyway, a court?"

"How about picking fights with Lazy JP riders?" Again Tobe changed his line of queries, hoping in the presence of Kazen to worm as much as possible from Soapy before rising anger forced him to seal his lips.

But Peggy answered. "My men have the strictest orders not to start a fight," she put in. "Nor molest your herds!"

Tobasco's eyes never left Soapy's face. "Can you back that up?" he taunted.

"Yes," growled the Horseshoe foreman. "I don't know of a time our men have ever started anything."

"Who started that fight in the Goldbug, you or me?" Tobe asked.

"You did!"

"You know that's a — you know better than that, Stevens!" Tobasco's tone was so low it was scarcely audible to the group around. "We'll pass it up however. But if I ever get anything on you or your men you'll go up for the limit. And don't ever get it into your head that you've heard the last of that fence deal either, by a long ways."

The open threat the words carried braced Soapy's lips in a thin grim line. Tobasco could see the implications in his stream of queries were firing a cold rage that presently would make the foreman either blurt out the truth — if indeed he knew — and defy the consequences, or retreat behind a mask of sullen silence.

Came to him again a wild impulse to bring up the murder of his father; to question Soapy as to whether or not he knew Two-Finger Brown. But again he decided to hold his tongue. There was absolutely nothing to connect Stevens with the slaying. His father had known Soapy. Had he been one of the trio, old Jackson would have recognized him. And if the Horseshoe foreman did happen to know Brown, or even know of his whereabouts he would only deny it. A question would reveal Tobasco's hand.

"Stevens, this feud is headed straight for the law courts," he found himself saying coldly. "When it gets there, I'm going to make a four-flusher out of somebody. Just remember that. As for you, Peggy," he told the girl, "I know you are not sanctioning every petty larceny move that can be made to cause trouble for the Lazy JP."

"Why . . ." she faltered, stubbornly refusing to meet his steady gaze. "I never have sanctioned any petty larceny moves, as you call them. What you —" She caught the slip. "Today was the first I knew of that state section lease."

"You didn't know that the Horseshoe has cornered every drop of water on the Lazy JP?"

"No. Why didn't you say something to me about it?" she demanded angrily of Stevens.

"I tried to tell you!" he flared. "You got bull-headed. There's no excuse for you getting on your high horse and hollering now because you didn't know."

Tobasco's fists clenched at the brutal tone. He took a step forward, but caught hold of himself quickly.

122

"Peggy!" He strove to keep out the caress that insisted on slipping into his voice when he addressed her. "As I told you before, my fight isn't against a woman. Unwittingly, you're a party to carrying on a feud that will wind up with a string of murders. More murders! . . . Murders that will shake the country if the thing is allowed to go on. I'm putting it up to you straight. As a lifelong friend of yours — of your uncle's — will the Horseshoe cancel its lease to that state section to enable us to renew ours so that we may also have water enough for our stock?"

He knew her answer would be yes. She started to speak. But Stevens answered for her.

"I reckon I've get a little something to say about that," the foreman sneered. "And I'm saying it. The Horseshoe ain't canceling that lease and you nor nobody like you can make us."

"You'll refuse at your own risk," Tobasco warned.

"You can't bluff me, you four-flusher in dude pants." Soapy laughed harshly. "All hell and high water can't make us cancel that lease. Now we've had our little pow-wow, you get your hoodlum wagons to moving . . . Pronto!"

"I'll move when I'm ready, Stevens!" Tobe shot back. "But you'll do some moving too. And the first move you make is this Horseshoe ranch-house. It happens to be just fifteen feet over the line onto my homestead."

"Your homestead!" Soapy yelled. "What the hell are you talking? Have you gone plumb loco?"

"Not half as crazy as you are for not canceling that lease," Tobasco grinned. "That artesian spring, which

123

supplies water for your stock, is on the section I just filed on. These other men have homesteaded every foot of ground around you. You're walled in. It isn't a question of us forcing you to give us an outlet to a county road — it's up to us to give you one. Now trot your men over there and get them to ripping down that fence from around government land. You've made your bluffs; now, damn you, back them up."

He stood spread-legged, his massive frame bulging with taut muscles, waiting for the stunned Stevens to speak.

"You can't file on our water and make us move our house!" the Horeshoe foreman blazed. "That ain't government land. So that's what those nosey surveyors have been doing on the Chimney Rock range lately?"

"Yep!" Kazen now enjoying the drama hugely, found his voice. "You finally stubbed your toe, Soapy. Tobe's had a re-survey of every foot of this ground. He's not only homesteaded your spring, but he owns fifteen feet of the ground your ranch-house is on. The proof has been put up to the authorities and okeyed. Got a court order right along with us. We don't want any trouble. But I'm here to tell you to snake down your fences, or a government man will do it for you. And let me tell you something else — the first time one of these homesteaders is molested, I'll know where to come for the walloper who is back of it." He roweled up beside the girl.

"Here's a package of papers your uncle left with me two or three years ago, Miss Peggy. Told me not to let a soul know I had 'em until after he was gone. Reckon

124

they belong to you now." He passed over a sealed envelope to the girl. She scarcely glanced at it, but stood with her face burning under the smile Tobasco flashed her as he started the caravan across the yard toward the spring beyond the ranch-house.

CHAPTER
FIFTEEN

Stevens stared darkly after the caravan until it had moved from sight behind the house. Then the grim mask that had veiled his seething emotions dropped from his face.

"Now what do you think of your sweetheart?" he hurled at Peggy, his furious gaze darting to the envelope Kazen had given her, and which she was crumpling in nervous fingers. "Reckon those papers have something to do with the ranch. I won't be partic'lar busy tonight. I'd better have a look through them . . . I'll turn them back to you in the morning."

She crushed the envelope behind her back. "No you won't," she defied him. "And as for Mr. Pepper," she said thrillingly . . . "I think he is smarter than either of us. As long as you have carried on this feud without my consent and knowledge — would not cancel that state lease, you secured through trickery, so his cattle can have water, I'm willing to suffer the loss just to see him whip you. And . . ." She spun about angrily and started away. ". . . If you'll notice, he doesn't have to carry a gun to do it, either."

126

An angry flush darkened his face. Leaping forward, he seized hold of her, spun her about and wrenched the envelope from her hand.

She recoiled, cheeks ashen. She started to speak. The fury on his face checked her. Stark fear possessed her. Willing to endure the loss rather than plead with the man, the very sight of whom now kept fired a consuming hatred within her, she turned and fled to the house.

Stevens rammed the envelope into his shirt pocket. Then through eyes that glinted fire, he strode to the corner of the house to stand watching the caterpillars as they walked awkwardly through the gate in the division fence and rolled down the gentle grade leading to the water-holes.

"What do you reckon they got them damned things for?" he demanded of a grizzled puncher who shambled up beside him.

"To farm that section." The man hastily straightened his smiling lips as the foreman half turned. "With all that water for irrigating, those tractors will bust out a pretty piece of fall wheat ground in no time. Besides, they'll scare all hell out of Horseshoe critters . . . So bad us cowhands can't get within a mile of them. Tough too, with beef roundup comin' on. Wish you'd of mentioned this before. I could of told you there was only a few sections old Jake was able to show patent to. The rest of his land is leased or open range, fenced back in the days when nobody wanted it."

"Is there . . . Honest to God is there a homestead open right there behind the house?" Soapy gulped.

"There's not only one, there's at least a half dozen of them. Just like Tobasco told you. But I reckon he's got it all cinched now. That walloper has got book l'arnin'. He's nobody's fool. If you'd of been smart you'd of took a tumble and got wise when all them surveyors got to prowling around, rerunning them lines."

Fury held Stevens mute. He fell to pacing about, blazing eyes glued on the caravan, which had halted a few hundred yards back of the big ranch-house. Not until the teamsters had started to unload the wagons did he stamp away toward the barn.

"We'll see about this," he muttered under his breath. "Damn his soul, I'll make him eat crow."

For an hour he beat a path between the barn and the ranch-house, cursing, kicking savagely at clumps of bunchgrass, tramping under foot delicate gumbo lilies. After a time he went to the bunkhouse to slump down on the steps and drag furiously on a cigaret. He looked up presently to see Sheriff Kazen leave the party, gallop through the Horseshoe, wave and shout to Peggy, then strike the road for Bigtrails. The sheriff's departure brought him to his feet to renew his savage pacing.

By evening, the skeleton of a shack had been erected on the corner of the section nearest the ranch-house. Stevens had climbed to the top of the round corral. With his spur rowels hooked into the poles his smouldering gaze was riveted on Tobasco and his group at work.

When the cook's stentorian voice announcing supper brought the punchers straggling to the house, he sat on, eyes fixed upon the moving arcs of fitful lantern light, ears deaf to all save the never-ceasing echo of hammers rearing a barbed barrier between the Horseshoe stock and water.

He climbed down presently and shambled to the house, master of the rage that boiled his blood; nor did the mask-like expression that now had settled on his face give a hint to what was churning in his mind. He slammed into the dining room, bolted his food in sullen silence, never glancing at the cowboys, who, it was evident, were bursting with eager questions.

When presently they all had finished, Soapy arose with them.

"There's a ten dollar raise in everybody's pay check starting today," he said significantly. "Heel yourselves heavy. Cram your belts and saddlebags with all the ammunition you can tote. We've got work to do. You, boy," he snapped at the wrangler. "Hustle down in the home pasture and shag up the cavvy. We'll want our top string horses tonight."

It was needless for the men to ask what he meant. His grim visage, the steely light in his eyes told them plainer than words. Those who had ridden for old Jake Elliot would have demurred. But for a thirty-dollar cowboy, an increase of ten dollars a month was not to be thrown aside lightly.

"Pretty risky business nowadays to drive a homesteader off his claim," one of the more intrepid ventured. "A break like that is monkeying with the United States government, you know!"

"To hell with the United States government!" Soapy blazed. "By the time anybody finds out about it, there won't be nobody left to squeal."

The men went outside to hang around in groups, speaking in low and guarded tones. After a time the cavvy, driven on a high lope by the cursing wrangler, pitched into the corrals. Stevens, who had remained behind, tiptoed to the foot of the stairs in a hallway adjoining, and listened a moment. He could hear Peggy pacing restlessly about in her chamber above. Removing his boots, in his sock feet he tiptoed to the second landing and turned the key in the lock. Ramming it into his pocket he descended and replaced his boots. As he started to leave the house, he collided with the cook.

"Naw, you don't, you rattle-hocked . . ." The cook barred the way, brandishing a knife. "I seen you lock that door, you sneaking . . . Supposing the place would catch a fire or something. Give me that key!"

Soapy's hand flashed to his forty-five. It leaped to the rim of its holster, stopped tight-pressed against his hip.

"I fired you once," he snarled. "Then let you stay to avoid a rumpus. You're so plumb eager to use that knife I reckon you'll come in handy tonight yourself. Make tracks for the corral."

The steady Colt warned the fuming cook against protest. Ahead of the threatening foreman, he strode from the house and stalked to the corrals where the others had their horses saddled. Unused to riding, softened by his years in the kitchen, he climbed onto a mount Soapy ordered rigged up, without a word. But the look he cast from narrowed watery eyes boded no good for the trailing Horseshoe foreman.

CHAPTER
SIXTEEN

The moon had not yet risen. Darkness lay like a pall over the prairies, Stygian darkness that defied sight, seemed to smother the faintest whisper of night life. Seated before a window in her bedroom, Peggy Elliot stared into the gloom. An unrest, a dread expectancy inspired by fear lay heavy on her soul. Of a sudden she roused herself, vaguely conscious of the vast quiet about the house and barns. The punchers usually were so noisy in the evening. Pulling her mind back from its idle wandering, she arose to investigate, stole softly to the door; turned the knob. The door refused to open. A sudden panic seized her. She rattled it. Still it resisted her. In desperation she tried to break the lock. The discovery that she was a prisoner fell upon her like a thunderbolt, giving rise to another wave of fear more terrible than those she had endured since Tobe and his caravan had pulled into the ranch. She had recognized the brutal glint in Stevens' eyes then. Now as she recalled them, she could read in their steely depths a scheme for vengeance. And that vengeance she knew would be swift and horrible.

She called to the cook. Softly first, then loudly, hysterically. The only answer was the echo of her own

132

voice slapping back at her from the walls of the room. She beat on the door until her clenched fists ached. Its sturdy panels mocked her puny attacks.

Crossing quickly back to the window, she threw it open and looked down. Below yawned a sheer drop of two stories onto the pithy wooden cover of the cistern, which supplied the ranch with drinking water. She remembered that cover of old. As a child she had broken through it. Only the timely arrival of her uncle in answer to her screams had saved her. The thought of that experience still haunted her like a nightmare. She drew away from the window fearfully. Escape by that means was out of the question.

"I've got to find a way," she whispered fiercely. "There must be some way."

She ran back to the door, seized the knob only to stop stock still, frozen in her tracks. A rattle of shots, from directly behind the house, had blasted the awesome quiet of the prairie, reverberated until it was a barely audible throb beating in the distance. When she could force herself to action, she stumbled back to the window, stark terror clutching her heart.

"Oh, God," she whispered reverently, "please save Tobe . . . for me. I've made a mistake, I know. But God . . . Don't let them kill him!"

Again a fusillade that seemed to freeze the blood in her veins. Fear loosed a flood of tears to fall unheaded across her cheeks. She buried her throbbing head in out-flung arms on the sill, straining with dread expectancy for another volley, which she knew would only strike new terror to her soul.

She dared another glance. A scream escaped her tight-set lips. A huge moon, swimming up over the eastern horizon suddenly had sprayed the prairie with a silver mist. The clumps of brush below her were alive with fingers of flame. Pale yellow powder flame, shot with tongues of red, laced the darkness as another broadside thundered out. She could hear the bullets splintering the skeleton of the newly erected homestead shack.

Came another silence, awful in its vastness that seemed to paralyze her. She moaned with helplessness. For the first time the meaning of the quiet that cloaked the bunkhouses crashed down upon her. Yet she stubbornly refused to believe her men were out there in the brush, fighting to kill the man she suddenly knew she loved with all her heart — had loved always.

She straightened up. Simultaneously, with a spurt of flame that ran along the bare rafters of the homestead shack, came the sharp "putt" "putt" of a barking motor. Astonishment for a moment held her motionless, straining to see. In the moonlight she made out the two caterpillar tractors. They were swinging their noses awkwardly about, lurching ahead. From the shelter of their hulks a volley roared out toward the men hidden in the brush. Something of a thrill passed through her. She could see the attackers slinking back, crawling to safety from these moving breastworks of steel, which came on across the brush, oblivious to the lead splattering their impenetrable hulls.

Muffled oaths reached her. Once she thought she heard Stevens cursing his men. But she was not certain.

Suddenly her body went rigid. Cold, numbing suspense held her upright as if waiting for death itself. The tractors had cleared the stretch between the blazing shack and the brush in which the besiegers lay. A big man, his height increased to gigantic proportions by the ghastly light, had leaped from the shelter of one tractor. With a forty-five streaking flame into the gloom ahead, he was leading the party into the face of the now scattered gunfire. She heard him above the barking of the engines.

"Give them hell, boys! We're in the clear now, fighting for our lives and property. There's not a court in the country which won't back us up!"

"Tobe! Tobe!" she shrieked into the thundering void. "Be careful! They're hidden right in front of you. Oh, God!"

The brush suddenly had upheaved in a roar of gunfire and tentacles of flame. She reeled, shut out the sight with her hands. But she must see. She dared another glance. Whether her scream had warned the advancing party, or whether they had seen the writhing forms, she did not know. But they had darted back to cover behind the tractors. Another sheet of flame split the gloom. A roar like thunder battered across the flats.

Overcome with emotion — stark terror intermingled with suppressed joy — she wilted to the floor. Clock-ticks passed, booming on her ears from the little timepiece on her dresser.

When she was able to drag herself from the grip of the awful lethargy that overwhelmed her, she was conscious only of silence. A stillness as vast as that found in chambers of the dead lay on the prairies; a stillness that seemed tangible; seemed to pierce her ears above the sluicing roar of her own hot blood.

She got dizzily to her feet, chilled with a sudden draught that sucked in from the flats to toss embers of the blazing shack aloft. She caught glimpses of shadowed figures, like wraiths, slinking from the brush. Below, at the corner of the house almost concealed in the creeping shadows, she made out a group of men. Low guarded voices, muffled curses, the creak of saddle leather drifted up to her. But she could not see their faces. Then they were gone into the night, the drum of running hoofs growing fainter, fainter, finally to become undistinguishable from the sound of her own racing pulse as she strained to listen.

Out by the spring the tractors had turned about, were crawling back. The piles of lumber had caught fire from the flying sparks. The silver moon was wan and pallid beside the awful glare. The pungent odor of smoke stung her nostrils. Suddenly she could make out Tobe's great form silhouetted against the fire. She leaned out to call to him, even though she knew he could not hear her. The words choked in her throat. A crackling drew her startled gaze upward.

The roof of the Horseshoe ranch-house was a seething mass of flame!

Her overburdened nerves threatened to snap under this new horror. Dully she realized she was trapped, locked in a burning house. Her eyes flew to the ground. A violent shudder racked her. More terrible at the moment was the Stygian depth of the cistern below than the blazing death above.

The room was filling rapidly with smoke, the open window sucking the flames nearer, nearer. She staggered to the door; beat wildly upon the panels. The smoke was suffocating her. The heat was unbearable. Stupefied with fear, she stumbled to her dresser. Her nervous fingers closed about the pearl handle of a little thirty-two. Holding her handkerchief over her smarting eyes and nose, she reeled back to the door, placed the muzzle of the revolver against the lock.

The roar of the shot made her ears ring. From force of habit she dropped the tiny gun into the pocket of her skirt. The door sagged open. She staggered back, clutching at her throat. A sheet of flame, new waves of smoke rolled in. Panic seized her. The window was her one hope. Rushing to it, she inhaled a deep breath which tore at her lungs, then crawled as far as she could on the narrow ledge and swung down arm's length. Sheer desperation gave her the strength to cling fast.

From out of an infinity of space she heard a clatter of hoofs. A hoarse shout. She clung on grimly, fearful to let go. Her fingers were growing numb. She sensed rather than saw two horsemen jerk up beneath her and leap to the ground. She struggled weakly to maintain her slipping hold on the ledge. She was falling. She waited dully for the splintering crash of the cistern cover. Then a deadening wave of blackness engulfed her.

CHAPTER
SEVENTEEN

Peggy's first conscious thought was of someone above her, stroking the hair back from her forehead, which felt parched and feverish. She knew she was lying down but she lacked the strength to open her smarting eyes. Cold water had been dashed in her face. She felt it trickling over her neck and shoulders. She lay panting, gasping for the air which shot sharp pains through her smoke-filled lungs.

"Peggy! Peggy!" came the voice of Tobe from far, far away. "For God's sake, Peggy!"

She managed to open her eyes, to meet his tortured gaze.

"I'll — be all right in a little while," she choked. "Oh, Tobe. I'm glad you're safe!"

The sudden tensing of his arms, which for a moment crushed the panting breath from her, meant more than words. Seemed to satisfy a longing that had haunted her for months. She was conscious of the pounding of his heart against her own. Spent as she was, she thrilled to his nearness.

Came the excited voice of the cook. "Poor little kid . . . She sure had a narrow shave. Stevens locked her in.

I tried to get the key. He threatened to plug me. The dirty cur!" Further than that, fear sealed his lips.

By the violent straining of the steel-like muscles about her, Peggy was aware of the wave of emotion the cook's words had aroused within Tobasco. Strangely happy in his arms, she lay, scarcely breathing, dreading the movement that would break the spell of contentment that enveloped her.

Another voice rudely interrupted her dreaming.

"Mr. Pepper!" The shout of a stranger, who had galloped up and thrown himself from his horse, caused her to start guiltily and attempt to free herself from the comforting arms. Tenderly Tobe lifted her to her feet. Unconsciously she nestled closer into the arm he threw protectively about her shoulder.

"Here I am," he said. "What is it?"

"All hell has broke loose!" panted the man, whom she now recognized as one of the six who had come in with the caravan that afternoon. "We followed the fellows who burned our shack. Down the road a piece we met a puncher riding like he was crazy. Said there was fifty armed men surrounding the Lazy JP . . . Name was Lonesome Harry. Said if I could find you to tell you he'd gone on for the sheriff and a posse . . . Told me to have you rouse every man you could and shag on down there, fast as you could . . . They'd had a fight in the afternoon on the state section. Later they were outnumbered. Chuckwallow, whoever he is, and his men were driven into the house."

Peggy's hand flew to her breast. "Who — who's doing it?" she asked.

"The Horseshoe!" Tobe blurted out bitterly. "Stevens! He's —"

He broke off, listening. The bark of distant gunfire drifted in on the breeze from the direction of the Chimney Rocks. "Where's your horse, Peggy?" he demanded.

"In the barn."

"Do you feel like riding?" A solicitous note crept into his voice. "I'm afraid to leave you here alone."

"I want to go — if you'll let me."

"Saddle Peggy's horse," he ordered the cook. "Get a move on you, too," as the man started to the barn on a walk.

Tobe whirled back to the homesteader who had brought Lonesome's message.

"Gather up the rest of our men. We'll head for the Lazy JP. It lays five miles due south. Just follow the road. You can't miss it. Miss — Mrs. Stevens —" He faltered on the name. "— and I will ride on. Catch up with us as quickly as possible." The man whirled his horse and galloped away.

Tobe's eyes swept the flaming house in one swift glance. "There is not much use in trying to save any of it, Peggy," he said grimly. "Besides . . . Chuckwallow and the boys need me."

"Never mind the house!" she cut in bravely, striving desperately to stifle the sob in her voice. "Help your men. It's been so — unpleasant here lately anyway . . . I don't care if I never see it again! Let's hurry."

The strength of resolute purpose drove her trembling legs to action. She sped for the barn, from which the

140

cook was leading her saddled pony, which snorted, and tried to lunge back from the flames. Then she was mounted and waiting impatiently when Tobe appeared from behind the house with his own wild-eyed plunging horse.

"See what you can do to keep the flames from spreading to the other buildings and the pastures," Tobasco shouted to the cook as he roweled up beside her. "I'll get help back to you as quickly as I can." Seeing she was ready, he lifted his pony into a pounding lope down the lane. She held the nervous bit-fighting brute while he undid the gate. Then side by side they raced down the road, a white ribbon in the eerie, ghostly glow that lit the flats.

She risked a glance over her shoulder. The ranchhouse was a cherry-red mass of embers. Uprights still stood, charred and burning. The fire was eating slowly into the brush. The shadow of the cook fighting grimly with blankets to hold it in check, danced unproportionate and grotesque against the lapping flames which lit the sky with a terrifying glow.

The scene loosed a flood of tears. It had been her home since childhood. Associated with it were lingering memories of freedom and happiness. And now it was gone. A cold rage settled over her; increased her hatred for Soapy Stevens . . . The man who had blasted her life and brought ruin to the ranch. With a sharp sigh, she turned back to meet the eyes of Tobe. He laid a hand over her's on the saddlehorn.

"Brace up, Peggy!" he said cheerfully. "There is plenty of lumber at Bigtrails — and maybe some day we —" He gazed at her mutely, his unfinished sentence as clear as though he had spoken.

"That's just it, Tobe," she choked. "If we . . . if I could look forward to . . ." She dropped her head to hide the tell-tale color that had surged furiously into her cheeks to set her throat pounding. ". . . being with you always." She finished in a tiny voice. "It wouldn't be so bad. But it's too late now. Oh, why did Uncle Jake do it?" The hopeless resignation in her voice brought a tense pressure from his fingers.

"There will come a day when we'll be together, Peggy . . . Just like we planned when we — were — kids," he whispered huskily. "This is bound to bring things to the showdown. You can move into Bigtrails for awhile . . . Until the thing has blown over. Then —" No need for her to wonder what he meant by his uncompleted sentence. Her heart, suddenly leaping to the pressure of his fingers, told her.

They pounded along in silence, their horses pushing distance behind them with amazing ease. Sage and greasewood loomed up about them like hideous vegetation of a nightmare. Shallow dry washes were bottomless chasms in the pale light. But always ahead lay the trail, chalk white in the moonlight. After a seeming infinity of time they crowded their blowing mounts up the side of the hogback overlooking the Lazy JP. She wondered at the fresh-turned mound beneath the rim-rock. But she asked no question. Nor could she see the gray-grimness that the sight of his father's grave brought to Tobasco's face.

142

Behind she could hear the thundering hoofs of Tobe's companions, who, having rallied, were coming on at breakneck speed. They slowed down, waiting for the others to come up. The scene below was quiet. Nothing moved. The brush loomed dark and fantastic in the moonlight. A peacefulness enveloped the flats as far as the eye could see. Yet the very hush was ominous. Behind the clouds of drifting smoke, the moon glowed a portentous red.

The homesteaders had scarcely reined their horses in beside them when powder flame laced the darkness, spurting from the arroyos around the ranchhouse. An instant later the report of the guns popped about them with startling clearness. Another hush. A half-hearted return of the fire from within.

"Good old Chuckwallow!" burst from the lips of Tobasco. "He's still holding the fort! Get as near as you can without being observed," he ordered the men in an undertone. "Then ride them down. Don't hesitate to kill!" Peggy shuddered at the deadly grimness of his mood. "They're shooting to kill — any man has a right to fight for his life and home. Peggy!" His voice dropped its harshness and became tender. "You stay here until you hear from me. It's too risky down there."

"Anything would be better than staying here alone," she pleaded. "Please let me go!"

He hesitated. "No," he said in a tone that brooked no protest. "You stay here."

Before she could reply, he roweled his mount down the face of the hogback and set a terrific, reckless pace for the others.

She sat her horse, sweeping the prairies. Behind, she could still see the fingers of flame reaching up into the sky from the burning Horseshoe; great billows of smoke tumbling lazily across the flats. She found herself wondering if the cook had saved the barns and bunkhouses; if the devastating flames were out of bounds and creeping out to destroy the range. She dared not think of her loss. The thought struck terror to her soul, made her choke on the sobs that filled her throat. Her utter impotence, the awesome loneliness which held her prey set her to trembling violently.

She pulled her gaze back to the scene below. The occasional rattle of gunfire added to the horror of the night. She straightened up in her saddle, taut, rigid. Tobe and his companions were but shapeless moving things. They had cleared the descent, were swinging in a detour toward the arroyo from which came the shots. She found herself praying aloud for his deliverance from harm, for an end to the feud which had turned the peaceful Chimney Rock range into a land of hatred and flaming lead.

To relax her twanging nerves, she shoved her hands into the pockets of her skirt and shifted sidewise in her saddle, weight in one stirrup. Her fingers came in contact with cold steel. Suddenly she remembered. She had brought her little thirty-two, with which she had shot off the lock of the door of her room during the fire.

She hesitated but a moment. Then she gave her pony rein. Its powerful strides, as it dashed recklessly down

144

the side of the hogback seemed to ease the tumult of her thoughts, for the moment satisfied the crying need of violence born of inactivity and helplessness.

CHAPTER
EIGHTEEN

Then almost before she realized that her madly running horse was down the slope of the hogback, was taking dry-washes and clumps of brush in great lunges, before the wind-stung eyes of Peggy Elliot rose up countless forms of men. The air was filled with whistling whining lead. The fingers of fire from the flashing guns stabbed the gloom like vivid streaks of lightning. She slashed her horse viciously with the quirt. It left the ground in a wild plunge, tore on across the brush. Girl that she was, the thrill of combat stirred her to the depths of her soul. Somewhere ahead, in the milling shooting mass, was the man she loved. Possibly another whom she hated. The blood that had won the spurs on the frontier trails for old Jake Elliot now hammered deafeningly in her ears.

"Drive them back!" she ground through gritted teeth. "Drive them back, Tobe!"

Then she was in the midst of the fray. She caught sight of Tobasco, urging on his men, his Colt spitting into the swaying, twisting crowd. She crowded her curveting horse to his side, thirty-two in her hand.

Surprised by the suddenness of the youth's attack, the besiegers had turned tail and fled. The homesteaders were after them, peppering the racing forms with lead. Wheeling, Tobasco glimpsed Peggy, white-faced, her thirty-two cracking, her prancing horse held in check with masterful skill.

"You have no business here, Peggy," he rebuked her sternly.

"Neither have you." She flashed him a smile in the moonlight, emptied her gun at the retreating forms.

"But as long as you are," he whispered in her ear, "give them hell — you wonderful, little — devil!"

He did not see the look that crossed her face, set tears to hovering on her lashes, for at that moment, sensing the sudden cessation of firing at the buildings to mean the unexpected arrival of reinforcements, the Lazy JP riders, Chuckwallow at their head, came tumbling from the house.

"Howdy, boys!" Tobasco yelled spurring forward to meet them. "What's coming off here? Who are they?"

"Must have been the Horseshoe," Grayson growled. "We didn't see a walloper that we could recognize." His eyes bulged at sight of the smoking Colt in the hands of the youth. A broad grin moved his mustache, spread over his wrinkled face. The other punchers crowded forward; a new note, that of the unreserved friendship they had given him in other days, in their voices as they greeted him. He gazed at them blankly, then down at the blue-barreled forty-five Kazen had insisted upon him keeping at the homestead shack. The meaning of their previous coldness burst upon him. The simple fact he would not carry a gun had caused the rupture of the old relations. He was glad in a way the wound had healed, yet the Colt in his hand cried opposition to all the tenets he had schooled himself to follow of late.

He found himself mumbling an apology, half to the men, half to ease his own accusing conscience.

He jerked his riotous thoughts back to hear Chuckwallow speaking.

"How many men does that damned outfit hire anyhow? There must have been fifty all told. We ought to chase these devils then ride over and blow that Horseshoe clean off the map. We —"

Catching sight of the girl, he stopped; flashed Tobasco a glance of surprise.

"How come she . . . How come Miss Peggy is with you?" he demanded blankly.

"Peggy doesn't know any more about it than we do," Tobe answered quickly. "She didn't even know there was a bloody range war on until I told her. She's as eager to settle the thing as we are. Peggy, have you hired any strangers on the Horseshoe lately?"

She shook her head. "I don't know of a single man that's new in the last two years," she replied.

"That's settled. They're not Horseshoe men, Chuckwallow. Where is Cateye Adams?"

"Sent him to town late this afternoon to wise you up hell had broke loose," Grayson answered. "Lonesome left this evening. Ought to be seeing something of Kazen pronto."

"Climb aboard your horses and let's run these fellows down!" Suiting his action to his words, Tobe drove the spurs into his own mount and raced in

148

pursuit of the gang. Peggy and the homesteaders thundered along close on his heels.

They halted presently, keeping the fleeing bunch in view while Grayson and the Lazy JP men caught up.

"Was anybody killed back there?" Tobe asked the foreman.

"I hope so," grunted Chuckwallow, "but I ain't had time to look. Long as it ain't any of our boys we'll do it in the morning. Where'd you come from?"

"We homesteaded the Horseshoe water-holes," Tobasco told him as he crowded his pony over beside the silent Peggy and the group started forward again. "I guess that is what started all this rumpus. It is all right for them to take our water, but when it comes to us taking theirs, of course, it's a different matter."

Chuckwallow shot the girl a suspicious look. "Had to ... That is ... Our stuff stampeded into the water-holes on the state section this morning," he ventured, reassured by the nod Tobe gave him. "We tried to stop them, but our herd got mixed with the — the other stuff. We offered to separate them ... The punchers guarding them got all het up and hostile. We had to shoot it out."

"Anybody hurt?" Tobasco demanded.

"Not as I know of. They drove us to shelter. Then a whole litter of the damned whelps come up. We didn't have no other course to follow but to hit for cover at the ranch — we'd been pecking at them off yonder in that arroyo for quite a spell before we broke. Lonesome rode through their fire to find you or the sheriff. They tried to down him, but he was too fast for them. And say —" Again he eyed the girl before speaking. "Them wasn't all Horseshoe critters they throwed into the state section the other day. A big part of them was Circle R's."

"Huh!" The exclamation of surprise burst from Tobe's lips. "That begins to clear things up. If we could just get our hands on one of those wallopers . . . We'd make him squeal or jerk his head clean . . ."

"Don't think for a minute we didn't give 'em every chance in the world to keep from fighting," put in Chuckwallow. "Lonesome, or any of the boys, will tell you we didn't start the ruckus . . . Didn't fire a shot until they opened up and we just naturally had to protect ourselves."

"Peggy," Tobasco addressed the girl abruptly. "Have you been losing any cattle lately?"

"Mr. — Stevens handles that," she replied. "He's reported lots of stuff straying but very little loss through rustling."

Apparently satisfied with her answer, Tobasco fell silent, his eyes riveted on the dim outline of the horsemen they were pursuing and who were now swinging into the hills behind the Chimney Rocks.

"Where do you suppose they are going?" Tobe asked.

"Looks like they're heading straight for the Circle R," Chuckwallow observed. "That spread's cabins lay back yonder a ways in that timber."

"I'll take a scout around there in the lead to be sure they don't give us the slip," Tobasco suggested.

"Let me go with you, Tobe?" whispered Peggy. "I'm — you know — the Lazy JP riders aren't friendly to me

150

any more. I can feel their antagonism. They — they look at me as though they thought I was here to spy. I'm afraid of them."

The youth smiled. "I'm only going in there a ways," he said. "But you can go with me if you want to." Then to Grayson. "We'll rejoin you fellows inside the next half hour. If we need help I'll fire three times in quick succession. If you don't hear my signal sit tight."

He turned a deaf ear to their protests. Motioning Peggy on, they rode ahead, the Lazy JP men watching them until they were lost from sight in a clump of jackpines.

"He's coming out of it in first class shape in spite of his pants and puttees," Chuckwallow remarked after a time. "Guess he ain't forgot how to use his gun, has he, fellers? The only thing now — I hate to see him teaming up with Peggy Elliot again until we get this mess settled. Not that she ain't a fine girl and all that, but ... Well, it's her fight and she's bound to have something to say around the Horseshoe. Say!" He sniffed the air suddenly, rigid in his stirrups, squinted eyes sweeping the flats. "Do any of you jaspers smell smoke?"

"It's the Horseshoe burning," volunteered one of Tobe's homesteaders. "Don't reckon there is much left of it by this time."

"The Horseshoe burning?" Chuckwallow blurted out.

"Yeah. We had a big scrap up there. They fired the shack we was building on Pepper's homestead. The Horseshoe ranch-house caught from the sparks and

151

burned down. The cook's back there alone, trying to keep the flames from spreading all over the range."

"There ain't no more Horseshoe ranch-house!" Chuckwallow exclaimed incredulously, now catching the eerie glow above the skyline to the north. "Say, that Tobasco is a wonder, that's all."

"Yep!" Red Maloney agreed. "And the best part of it is, you can bet the ace he ain't done a thing to get the Lazy JP in dutch with the law. Him homesteading them Horseshoe water-holes is the best — strategy I every heard of."

"Always said he had brains," Chuckwallow returned proudly.

"Why, you bow-legged old bullbat, you've knocked him harder than any man on the place," Red grunted. "You said he ought to been hung and quartered for not doing what his paw asked him to."

"Go to hell!" Grayson growled savagely. "He's doing it, ain't he?"

The question would admit of no argument. Then, as the situation was pregnant with possibilities for an open break, they all fell silent and started moving slowly ahead, pausing from time to time to listen.

"It looks to me as though things are coming to a showdown fast now, Peggy," Tobe said in a guarded tone. "I had hoped to settle it without bloodshed . . . But I guess it can't be done."

"There is no use in letting it worry you," she answered. "You're not to blame. We're into it now — we can't turn back — we've —"

152

Her sentence was never finished. Directly in front of them, the men they were trying to head off had detached themselves from the trees. Before Tobasco could fire the signal to his riders, he and Peggy were surrounded.

"Don't shoot," Tobe said quickly. "There's a girl here with me."

"Don't mind me," Peggy whispered fearlessly.

"Then throw down your iron," came a gruff voice.

Tobasco hesitated for a moment. The girl's words had sent the blood of recklessness again to pounding in his temples. He sized up the gang in a single glance. The odds were too great. Even as he paused, a bullet "pinged" past his ear. The song of hate it sung turned his blood to ice. The drumming of hot blood became a sluicing roar in his ears. Yet he hung onto himself grimly, unwilling to expose Peggy to needless danger. He tossed his Colt to the ground. A second gun spoke.

"There's my forty-five!" he shouted. "I'm not fighting back. Put up your guns unless you want to kill Peggy Elliot of the Horseshoe."

The effect was electrical. A half dozen men leaped forward. From the corner of his eyes, Tobasco glimpsed a rambling log building tucked far back in the trees.

"Well, I'll be darned, Peggy," he exclaimed, seeming to give no thought to his capture, "I'll bet this is the Circle R and we rode right into it."

Before he could catch her reply a stunning blow on his head from behind sent him pitching forward in his saddle. A suffocating mantle of blackness overwhelmed him.

153

CHAPTER
NINETEEN

Nightfall found Bigtrails in the grip of wild excitement. Yet for all of it the village was strangely quiet. Punchers gathered in knots along the dimly lighted street, engaged in low-voiced conversation. Punchers squatted on their heels in darkened doorways, spinning their spur rowels with nervous fingers. A few even had secured their horses, slunk down the alleyways and headed out for the open country.

Broncs pounded the length of the narrow street, each newcomer drawing every gaze. Green broncs which cowered trembling at the noise, lined the hitchrails. The atmosphere itself was surcharged with an electric tenseness, which seemed to be felt by man and beast alike.

Up in the Goldbug the excitement was at fever pitch. The arrival of Cateye Adams a short time before with word of the fight at the water-holes had created a furore. In this new crisis, so close upon the unsolved murder of old Jackson Pepper, Cowland sensed the arrival of the final showdown between the Lazy JP and the Horseshoe, which they long had felt, with dread expectancy, must surely come.

Unable to locate Tobasco, Cateye had summoned Joe Kazen. The sheriff had stopped for a moment at the Goldbug to relate the meager details of the affray as he had them from Cateye before riding out of town. The word flew from mouth to mouth. Bigtrails waited for word of the explosion.

But not for long did they have to wait. Scarcely had the first flush of excitement died down and the fiddle in the honky-tonk resumed its scraping, when a burst of hoofbeats in the street warned of new developments. Punchers craned for glimpses of the riders. Few men pounded horses at such terrific paces unless the need was urgent.

Three dusty-garbed men pulled rein at the Goldbug, threw themselves from their saddles and strode inside. Everyone trooped along. It was Kazen again. With him was Cateye Adams and Lonesome Harry Sager. The sheriff's tale was brief. He had covered but a few miles of the trail to the Lazy JP when he had met Lonesome, fanning his winded horse in a desperate effort to reach town with the report of the siege of the ranch-house before the trembling animal's sweat-smeared legs gave out.

Lonesome's panted message had turned Kazen and Cateye back. The three had raced into Bigtrails. Convinced now was Kazen that the flare-up they had feared for months had finally come. And he was not slow-witted enough to believe that he could cope with it single-handed. Yet he was in a quandary. With the town packed with strangers, old-timers cautious and close-lipped about their leanings, collecting a posse would be no easy matter. He recognized the need of a number sufficient to overwhelm the combatants quickly, if a pitched battle was to be avoided. He took the one course open. The Goldbug.

"It's war at last," he shouted hoarsely to the group, as old Ivor Johnson, straining not to miss a sound, caromed bottles and glasses across the bar. "Hell's broke loose. First the scrap at the waterholes on that Lazy JP state section. Cateye brought word of that. Now Lonesome runs the gauntlet to tell me they've got old Chuckwallow Grayson and his men holed up in the Lazy JP and shooting all hell out of them."

"But Tobasco," Johnson put in. "There was a time when — where's Tobasco?"

"Supposed to be either here in Bigtrails or some wheres with a surveyin' . . ." Lonesome essayed as he gulped his drink and reached for the bar bottle.

"I left Tobasco at the Horseshoe yesterday afternoon," Kazen said. "He homesteaded . . ." He caught himself up quickly. "The Lord only knows where he is now — all hell's to pay. We've got to stop it. I'm deputizing you jaspers."

"Hold on a minute." Johnson leaned across the bar and spoke in a guarded tone. "You ain't fool enough to deputize any of these strangers hanging around here, Joe. Besides, you don't know what they'll do under gunfire, like as not run like the devil. There ain't enough he-men in the place to be a drop in the bucket if the Horseshoe and Lazy JP have gone to steel. No sir — that's a job that'll take real cowhands — not tinhorns. Hell, an army of these jailbirds —"

156

"But what we goin' to do," Kazen demanded blankly. "If they're shootin' they've gone too far for me to stop 'em without help."

"I know what I'm going to do," Lonesome, having slaked his thirst put in. "I'm going to feed my face. I haven't et for so long —"

"Throw it into you and make it fast," Kazen snapped. "And you too, Cateye." He lowered his voice to Johnson. "What the devil are we going to do, Ivor? It's either deputize a bunch big enough —"

"Why not get Captain Mason to call out the militia?" the bartender suggested. "You know what war between them two spreads mean! Man, it's a real blow-up — Nothing for a handful of men to try and —"

"That's an idea." Kazen dashed off his drink and started for the door. "I'll be back pronto, Lonesome," he shouted to the two Lazy JP men who had shambled over to the lunch counter and dropped wearily onto stools. "Wait here for me." He strode through the swinging doors into the night. A sudden clatter of hoofs announced his departure.

Off into an unlighted street he plunged to jerk rein before a darkened house.

"Captain Mason!" he shouted in a voice that brought the commander of the local troop of National Guard Cavalry to the door on a run. "All hell has broke loose on the Chimney Rock range. Lonesome Harry just brought in word. They're fighting a big battle now. They've got Chuckwallow and the Lazy JP men surrounded in the Lazy JP ranch-house. I can't

157

organize a posse I can depend on. Can't you call out your troop?"

"Sorry, Joe." There was sincere regret in the officer's voice. "I have no authority to muster my company for any such thing as that. Do the best you can at rounding up a posse. I'll wire the adjutant general and the governor immediately to see what I can do."

"A hell of a fine bunch of soldiers we're paying to lay around here!" Kazen exploded. "What are they for anyhow?"

The darkness hid the angry flush on Mason's cheeks. "Don't worry. The State will take care of it when it gets bigger than a one-man job."

"Bigger than a one-man job with the Horseshoe and Lazy JP twisting tails with forty-fives!" the sheriff roared. He jerked his bit-fighting horse about. "Keep your tin soldiers. I'll stop this damned range war so quick it'll make their heads swim. I'll learn 'em whose running this county. And I won't need none of your soldiers to do it, either!"

He lifted his horse with the rowels and was gone in a cloud of dust, leaving the captain white-faced with rage staring into the darkness after him.

Kazen's first stop was at the Goldbug. Luckily, now the saloon was crowded, citizens and cowhands alike crowding in for word of the battle. Kazen's cry for volunteers brought every man in the place to his feet. But it was a grizzled old cowhand who once had ridden with Jackson Pepper who cinched the response.

"Is Tobasco in trouble?" he demanded loudly.

For the first time, Lonesome, devouring a steak smothered with onions, at the rear of the resort, remembered what the stranger he sent in search of Tobe had told him. "Hell, yes!" he roared. "There's a big battle on at the Horseshoe too — I plumb forgot that in all the excitement, Joe," he apologized. "There was a fire down there, too. It looked like the whole ranch was burning up as I come by."

"Fire — fight at the Horseshoe, too," Kazen muttered.

"Hell —"

"That's enough," Johnson snarled, stripping off his apron, buckling a forty-five about his ample waist, and dragging on his coat. "The joint is closed for the night, fellows. Come on, everybody. Tobasco needs help!"

They trooped out to a man, although it was obvious that many were decidedly reluctant to mix into the range war. But with no place to go, except to bed now that Johnson had locked the door behind him, they had no alternative. Those who did not have horses descended on the livery barn in a medley of shouts and curses. In short order the stable was emptied of its mounts. Scarcely thirty minutes had elapsed when Kazen, with Lonesome and Cateye at his side, led the party from town toward the Chimney Rocks.

The long trail was eaten up at an amazing pace. The group was singularly silent, speaking only at intervals and then in low voices.

At the Horseshoe when they galloped up they found the ranch-house a pile of glowing ruins. The smudgy-faced cook, who, aided by a shifting wind, had succeeded in keeping the flames from the bunkhouses and barns, sat on the parched ground mopping his forehead and staring through bloodshot eyes at the smouldering heap that had been his home for twenty years.

"Don't mind me," he shouted hoarsely, recognizing Kazen and leaping to his feet as the posse thundered up. "There's nothing you can do here. The old ranch is done for. Bust the breeze for the Lazy JP. There's been hell popping down there for the last three or four hours. And Joe," he yelled as the officer whirled his leg-weary mount about, "keep your eye peeled for Peggy. She's with Tobasco."

Again the posse was on the trail. But now its speed was slackened. The acrid smell of smoke that clung to the humid air filled them with apprehension. The smouldering Horseshoe chilled them. Fire is the greatest fear of Rangeland.

There was no sign of life in the huddled buildings of the Lazy JP as they put their horses up the slope and down the hogback without slackening their rapid pace.

"Now what the hell are we up against?" Kazen broke the sphinx-like silence in which he had been wrapped since they left the Horseshoe. When no answer was forthcoming, he got down and fell to pacing about nervously. After a time the rattle of wheels drifted up the valley. Swinging aboard, Kazen stood in his stirrups, the possemen tense beside him. A light wagon hove in sight, careening toward the ranch-house behind galloping broncs.

"Don't shoot unless I say so," he warned. "We'll take a look at that fellow who is in such a hurry. Then we'll decide what we're going to do."

At sight of them the driver swung about. With his cracking lash straightened across the backs of his lathering team, he tried to elude them. But at a word from Kazen, the posse swooped down upon the wagon.

"Where you going in such a rush?" Kazen shouted, leaning over in the saddle and seizing a cheek-piece.

The teamsters did not reply. He sat staring in stupefaction at the group.

"I said whose wagon is this and where you going in such an all-fired hurry?" repeated the sheriff.

CHAPTER
TWENTY

But the driver might have been deaf for all the answer he made to Sheriff Joe Kazen's thundered question. He sat peering at them through the wan light of a moon hanging low above the western horizon. He twisted uncomfortably but refused to talk. Kazen got down, lighted a match and peered into the wagon box.

"Hell's Bobcats!" he cried, extinguishing the flame quickly. "It's dynamite!"

He whipped out his gun. "Who owns that stuff?" he barked, bounding around the wagon and throwing down on the surly driver.

"The Circle R!" At sight of the Colt the sullen driver found his voice.

"And who owns the Circle R?" Kazen shot back.

The teamster shook his head. "I don't know. They told me to go to the ranch and get a flock of dynamite, they'd been using to dig post holes. I did. That's all I can tell you."

"Who are they?" Kazen demanded.

"The Circle R men who were shooting up the Lazy JP."

Before the angry officer could give vent to surprise at the discovery that Circle R men and not the Horseshoe,

162

were attacking the Lazy JP, a rattle of shots came from the hills.

It brought the men rigid in their saddles. Kazen strained, listening.

"Dynamite!" he exploded. "They sure was allowing to go strong. Here, you hoot-owl," he flung at the driver, "drag those nags of yours around. Head straight toward the brakes and that firing. We'll be camping on your trail and we'll drop you if you try any monkey business. Come on, boys. If we're playing with a gang of jaspers who are ready to use dynamite to blow up the Lazy JP, I reckon it's time for us to unlimber our smoke poles and give them as good as they aim to send."

Quietly tipping off Lonesome and Cateye to hang back with the teamster to see that he did not attempt to escape, the officer and his posse galloped in the direction from which the sound of gunfire had come.

The broken country now forced slower going. But after a time they glimpsed a group of men skylined above them. Chuckwallow galloped fearlessly down to challenge them. He let out a war-whoop when Kazen spoke.

"Right glad to turn the thing over to you, sheriff," he grinned, swiping blood-shot dust-rimmed eyes. "Us fellows have had about all the fighting we want for one day. What's happened to Lonesome and Cateye?"

Kazen told him. "Who's houses are them over yonder?" He peered through the wan light at the outline of rambling log buildings.

"That's the Circle R," Grayson said. "There must be fifty of them hombres in there. They shot up the Lazy

JP, then run for it when Tobasco hit them like a cyclone from behind. They captured the kid and Peggy I guess, because we ain't been able to locate them."

"Know any of them?" questioned Kazen, studying the place, which resembled a barricaded fortress with rifle barrels glinting from cracks in the 'dobe chinking of the logs and from which an occasional shot laced flame into the gloom.

"Nary a one," Chuckwallow returned. "But they're the hardest looking hoot-owlers I ever run across outside of any pen."

"You say Tobasco is a prisoner?" Johnson demanded, pushing his horse into the center of the group.

"As far as we know, Ivor, he is. Him and Peggy — you know — Peggy Elliot. Oh, they've buried the hatchet, I guess," Chuckwallow added as a puzzled look flashed across the face of the bartender, to whose mind returned a picture of the youth's encounter with the girl the day he arrived in Bigtrails. "Anyhow, Tobasco started to head them wallopers off. He was to fire three times if they needed us. Told us not to follow unless we heard three shots. We heard two shots. Then everything got quiet. Later somebody blazed away at us from the house, so I reckon the kid and gal's been took. We been kind of laying low here augerin' the best thing to do and waiting for better light."

"Well, it's a cinch we won't get nowhere standing around like this," Kazen observed in a business-like tone. "Do you reckon there's enough moonlight left so's they could see a flag of truce?"

Chuckwallow squinted to the west. "Yep," he answered. "That is if anybody's fool enough to try and go up there with one."

The officer did not reply, but calmly uncoiled the lariat at his saddle horn and tossed it over a clump of brush. Uprooting it, he dragged a kerchief from his pocket. Attaching it to the brush, he raised it above his head. They waited a few minutes. The sniping ceased. An answering splash of white appeared in front of one of the buildings.

"You fellows stay here," the sheriff warned, spurring forward alone. "I'll take care of this thing myself. I want to find out just where the Circle R stands in this row and how much hell these fellows are able to take before they are ready to give up the ghost."

He rode forward. The party strained after him. Presently they saw a stranger come out into a clearing, his flag of truce waving aloft.

"Well?" demanded the fellow in a booming voice that carried back plainly to the waiting group.

"Well yourself!" the officer snapped. "I'm Joe Kazen, sheriff of this county. Who are you and what is the meaning of all this trouble?"

"It's none of your business who I am," the man threw back. "As for what the trouble is about, them Lazy JP jaspers tore down the division fence between their pasture and that state section the Horseshoe has got leased. And their cattle stampeded and got mixed with our critters."

"What business you got with your stuff on the Horseshoe lease?" Kazen demanded.

165

"We got permission to throw a bunch in on the water-holes."

"Who give you permission?"

"I reckon we don't have to tell everything we know to run cattle on this range, do we?" the fellow snarled. "Is there any law against arranging to get water for your thirsty stock?"

The evasive reply angered Kazen. "Who owns this Circle R outfit anyway?" he exploded. "Looks like a damned hoot-owl spread to me. Come through, or I'll pump you full of holes."

"Hop to it!" the man taunted, ignoring the question, but taking up the challenge. "My men there in the cabins are just itching for you to start something out here. Then again, from the heft of you, I don't reckon I'd need any reinforcements. But you'll probably need all you can muster. I didn't know you come in under a flag of truce for a gunfight — but you'll sure as the devil get one if you've got any hankering thataway."

Kazen swelled up angrily. "Never seen no hootowler yet who could run a whizzer on me. I ain't scared of you or your whole gang. I'm telling you in the name of the law to throw down your guns and come out of there. If you don't, I've got enough men to surround the place. I got a hold of that dynamite you figured to blow up the Lazy JP with. Now, damn you, talk turkey or I'll blow this dump from hell to breakfast. You can begin by trotting out Tobasco Pepper and Peggy Elliot."

"You're talking plumb foreign to me when you talk names I don't know," the fellow retorted fearlessly. "We ain't got no Tobasco Pepper, sauce or — nor gal in that

166

cabin either. As for you blowing us up, fly to it if you feel lucky." He took a threatening step forward, his thumb of his gun hand hooked in his cartridge belt.

Back at the posse, Chuckwallow saw the move. Itching for action, the old fellow shouldered his carbine. It cracked. The bullet plowed a furrow at the stranger's feet.

"See," the fellow blazed, lurching back. "That's the kind of men you've got behind you. Breaking a truce. Now, damn you, travel and travel fast. This pow-wow is over. We'll scrap it out!"

Livid with rage, the sheriff wheeled his horse and galloped back to the waiting men. "I don't know who fired that shot," he growled, "but whoever it was sure did me just plenty of a favor. Open up and blow the devil right out of that gang of rannyhans."

The nervous men needed no second invitation. Instantly the guns along the line spoke in a deafening broadside. The bullets threw a sheet of dust over the ranch-house. An answering volley came from within.

But in the fading light of a swiftly sinking moon the firing was useless for destruction. It only served as an outlet for pent up nerves. After the first few rounds they settled down to steady sniping, which continued through the night. One by one the remaining splinters of glass were found in the single window by random lead. And many of the horses, snorting in terror in the corral behind the building, were killed.

In the hours of early morning the incessant firing began to tell on the ammunition supply of the possemen. They fell back from range for a conference.

"I'm plumb satisfied Tobasco and Peggy are in there," Kazen said. "I'm going to get them or give up the ghost trying. But we can't do it with this long range shooting. If we used the dynamite, like as not we'd blow the kids up with the rest of them galoots. Tell you what we could do. We could plant the stuff near enough to blast a trench right under their noses. It would scare all hell out of them, too. Where's that wagon?"

Lonesome, who had piloted in the wagon and had the cowering driver in tow, led Kazen to the vehicle which had been left in the shelter of a wash a short distance back.

"Who's game to go with me to plant it?" Every voice arose in answer to Kazen's question. "All right then. Save your cartridges. We'll run them hombres out with their own medicine."

The moon scudded from sight below the horizon. Pre-dawn darkness settled down in a Stygian blanket over the flats. Under its protecting cover Kazen and Chuckwallow crawled toward the building. About half way, the sound of hoofs halted them. Raising himself cautiously, the officer peered about.

"Might as well go back," he growled in an undertone. "It's a whole flock of riders. Reckon it's Mason and his tin soldiers — now that we don't need them." They made their painful way back through pricking sage and cactus beds. And Kazen's conjecture proved correct. No sooner had they rejoined the posse than the troop of cavalry from Bigtrails galloped up.

"I'll take charge now, Joe," announced Captain Mason officiously. "I wired the governor after you left.

I've been ordered to force the arrest of every man implicated in this feud."

"It's about time your tin soldiers did something," Kazen muttered. "'Lowed you'd come just as quick as I had a way figured out to rout 'em. The hombres you want are in that Circle R ranch-house there, fifty strong. From what the Lazy JP boys tell me, you sure got here in time. A few minutes more and I'd of scared them all to death. I'd of made them call quits."

The officer looked at the explosive and smiled. "We won't need that dynamite," he said. "I'll go in under a flag of truce with daylight. I don't want to use force if it can be avoided. But I'll tell them where to head in."

Kazen studied him coolly for a moment. "Are you really talking what you think or are you trying to convince us what a fine bunch of soldiers you are?" he snorted contemptuously.

The officer drew himself up with dignity. "Wait and see how we handle this little affair."

"Well, all I can say is that you've got a heap to learn about hunting tough jaspers like them yonder," Kazen retorted sarcastically. "And what's more, if you get near that house with a flag of truce, or any other way, you'll be plumb lucky."

A suppressed chuckle from Johnson and Chuckwallow sent the fuming captain back to his troop. The cavalrymen dismounted and settled themselves to wait for dawn. The darkness thickened. The vast and ominous silence found in chambers of the dead settled down; a silence broken only by the cough of a nervous hoofed pony and the thin whisper of night life.

CHAPTER
TWENTY-ONE

To the roar of gunfire, which beat horribly on his ear-drums with its nearness, Tobasco groped slowly back to consciousness. The first lucid thought of which he was fully aware was of a spinning head that ached fearfully. His throat and tongue were parched. His lips felt too swollen to open. His whole body was afire, a bundle of throbbing, twitching nerves. His nostrils stung with the pungent odor of powder smoke that hung thick about him.

He lay for a time without moving, his logy muscles refusing to respond to his will. Then when he had managed to get a grip on his faculties he attempted to ease his cramped position. The effort was painfully futile. He was bound hand and foot. His movement only drew the pieces of rope tighter into his flesh.

By the pale rays of moonlight filtering through a paneless window he could make out several men about a large room, faces evil and leering as they laid against the stocks of barking rifles. Save for an occasional inspection of his fetters, they paid no attention to him, but, in a cold, heartless way, stuck to their task of throwing shell for shell with an attacking party.

It was an awesome, deadly pantomime; the stillness broken by the crack of guns, the metallic click of ejectors, the shuffling of feet and the "ping" of bullets that chipped the 'dobe from between the logs or buried themselves with a dull thud in the outer walls.

Suddenly he figured the thing out in his muddled mind. No longer were they at the home ranch. Chuckwallow had turned the tables, had the Circle R surrounded. With this first coherent thought, came fear for Peggy's safety. She had been with him, but — he strove to locate her. Even after his burning eyes had become accustomed to the darkness he could not penetrate it.

Outlined above him for a moment was a burly form.

"Where's the girl?" he demanded in a voice that startled him with its weakness.

"Keep your mouth shut!" came a surly warning.

Tobasco struggled against a cold fury that turned his soul to ice, set scalding blood to hammering in the open wound on his head. Knowledge that Peggy had been made a captive by these ruffians set him to new and hopeless straining on his fetters. Presently, realizing the need for coolness, he quieted down and lay trying to bring order from the chaos of his mind.

An endless train of riddles stalked before him. What did his captors intend to do with him? What connection, if any, did they have with the Horseshoe? Was the man who had killed his father even now among those about him? Was one of the group the man who had tried to murder him? Who paid the wages of this death-dealing gang which had driven the Lazy JP riders to shelter in the ranch-house? That they were Circle R men was evident, yet he could not believe the Circle R would employ such a number of gunmen — for that gunmen they were he could tell by their stoical grimness and the occasional muffled curses when a shot went wild. He tried to pick the leader from the shadowed figures. But everyone seemed like the next.

Were they part of the crowd which had attacked his homesteaders and burned his shack? Had they meant to raze the Horseshoe ranch-house and kill Peggy, or was it for some other purpose she had been made prisoner in her room? The cook had told him Stevens locked the door and pocketed the key. In the face of that statement, it appeared that Soapy was deliberately plotting her death, else why had he not released her?

The last question set his quivering nerves on edge. Perhaps Stevens was in league with these gunmen and, having failed to kill Peggy had left it to the gang whose prisoner she was.

The fear drove all else from his tortured mind. He must find a way to escape. But hope sank as it was born. Guarded by no less than twenty-five men with rifles in hand, his chances were less than nothing.

Suddenly the firing ceased. One of the men strode across the room, threw open a door. For a full minute he stood outlined in the moonlight. Something about the figure struck Tobasco as vaguely familiar, but the fellow slammed the door and left the house before he could recognize him.

Minutes passed; tense, palpitating minutes during which the gang stood with ears pinned to the cracks in the 'dobe, scarcely moving.

Came a sudden shot. The man leaped back into the house. The firing was renewed. To the tune of whining lead, Tobasco settled down to scheme some way, if possible, to make an escape.

"The soldiers!" A whisper, that ran 'round the group after an infinity of time, brought him rigid. "It's too dark to see. But I can hear a bunch of horses and metal clinking. Let's get going while the going is good."

A new ray of hope was born to Tobe in the disclosure. It faded quickly. Heavy hands laid hold of him. His head was twisted around. A filthy gag was crammed between his cramped jaws. They lifted him up roughly. He tried to worm from their grasp, fought with every ounce of his wasted strength to raise a commotion that would warn Chuckwallow and his men. But his efforts only brought another blow on the head from the butt of a forty-five. The black cloud of insensibility again engulfed him.

A murky gray replaced the black on the eastern horizon. Then pink tinged the sky; shifted like the borealis and deepened into red. Fanlike streamers of yellow flame reached up over the hills.

When it was light enough, Captain Mason went forward under a flag of truce. But, this time, there was no answering signal from within. Taking courage from the silence, the officer ordered up the troop. The cavalrymen gained the house without challenge; surrounded it. Guns in hand, the posse sprang inside. Chuckwallow at their head.

"They've flew the coop!" bawled the foreman of the Lazy JP.

Mason strode within, uttered an exclamation of surprise. The gang had disappeared! The sighing of the wind in the densely-timbered hills and the champing of the bits in the horses' mouths were the only sounds that broke the oppressive stillness.

Dawn lifted in a fling of vivid color along the rim of the hills. The sun came swimming up in a sea of metal brilliance to set the blistered prairies dancing like a mirage. A search of an hour revealed only a bewildering maze of criss-crossed trails leading in every direction. Hoof prints there were none. The wearied group sat down presently for a consultation.

"I'll have to be getting back to Bigtrails," Mason informed Kazen. "I have no orders to engage in a man hunt. I was detailed to call out my troop only to arrest the men who were the cause of all the trouble." He looked along the row of haggard faces. "I'm going to leave it to you to arrest the ones in your party who are mixed up in the affair."

"You'll never get 'em," answered the sheriff. "Nor you won't get Tobasco if we find him. I know these men, every mother's son of 'em, and a lot of them have took more than either you or me would have took." His tone changed. A worried note crept into his voice. "Wish to God we could locate Tobe. I'm not just what you'd call used to hunting armies. And I don't know just how many I'm entitled to kill off under the law."

"You are invested with the power to bring the law-breakers to justice," the captain said. "You can press into service as many deputies as you consider necessary. You have the right to arrest any man you have good cause to suspect. If he resists, that is his look-out. I don't believe you need an attorney along."

Kazen glared at him belligerently. "Is that so?" he blurted out. "I'm sure glad for your pointers on how to be a sheriff. Thanks, too, for the good work you done in locating the house where those fellows had been. Reckon while I think of it — seeing as you have orders to arrest any man connected with this thing — I'll tell you here and now; every man in my posse is a deputy sheriff. And Tobasco is a deputy sheriff. If he's killed about sixteen of those wallopers when the thing's over, he was shooting in the name of the law. Now what do you think of that?"

Mason's reply was a sharp order which set his troop in motion along the back trail. Grinning broadly, the sheriff watched them until they dropped from sight in a ravine. Then he turned back to his waiting men.

"Reckon we better eat somewheres, deputies," he chuckled. "Let's lope on down to the Lazy JP and have the cook sling us together some grub. I'm bettin' we can figure just a whole heap better on a full stomach."

CHAPTER
TWENTY-TWO

An hour or a day might have elapsed, for all Tobe knew, before he again pierced the dark wave that enveloped him. Slowly his senses returned. His first conscious thought was one of great relief. Presently he discovered the cause of it. The suffocating gag had been taken from his mouth. But he was still bound hand and foot. And the blood still pounded with sickening regularity in the wound on his head.

As his pain-dulled eyes became accustomed to the gloom, he gazed about. Feeble rays of sunlight, straggling through the cracks in the chinking of the logs barring an entrance, strove to pierce the obscure, foul-smelling interior, which, by the precipitous rock on either side, he knew was a great cave. The soot of many a camp-fire clinging to the walls gave evidence that the place was some sort of a rendezvous.

Stretched on his back, he wriggled his cramped body about on the dirt floor until he was able to turn on his side and see behind him. Some inherent sense of danger warned him to caution. At the far end of the cavern two men sat on the floor, sleeping, their backs braced against the wall. The light from a smoking lantern revealed but a half of their evil faces. The other side was hidden in the shadows that danced grotesquely in the wan and flickering light.

Wondering what had become of their companions, Tobasco lay studying them through half closed eyes. The larger of the two, he decided, was the man who had left the cabin during the lull in firing. He had stirred a vague sense of familiarity within him then. And now again Tobasco felt that he was someone he had known or seen.

As his scattered wits returned and his nerves steadied somewhat, a flood of questions began crowding into his bewildered mind. But he put them aside, suddenly harassed with fear for Peggy's safety. He hesitated to waken the two, yet in his anxiety for word of her he could not remain silent any longer.

"Where's Peggy!" he demanded in a thick unnatural voice. "You'd better be sure she's not harmed!" The echo slapping back from the bare walls revealed to him how utterly puerile the words sounded.

The smaller of the two men bolted to his feet, gun in hand. The other only stirred, opened his eyes, then, with a cool carelessness which stamped him as a man devoid of fear, he settled himself more comfortably against the wall to continue his nap.

"Never mind the gal!" snarled the little fellow, coming quickly to Tobe's side, his footsteps scarcely audible on the sand floor. "You can be thankful we haven't bumped you off instead of toting you around with us. We all got hell for not croaking you once before. Now lay quiet or I'll bust you with my forty-five again!"

The intimation that it was this gang which had tried to kill him at the Lazy JP sent an involuntary shudder through Tobasco. But a growing suspicion that one of them was the slayer of his father steadied him instantly.

"Reckon that would be just about your caliber — hitting a man bound hand and foot, you coyote!" he threw back recklessly. "I'm warning you, that girl had better be safe when I get loose or —"

"When you get loose?" his captor leered at him. "Say, jasper, by the time you get loose you'll have forgotten her name even. Now shut your yawp!" He glared savagely at Tobasco, his beady little eyes gleaming in the lantern light. But the pain, the constant thought of Peggy, and his helplessness to solve the baffling chain of problems now churning crazily in his mind fired Tobe with an utter disregard of consequences.

"I'll keep quiet when I get damned good and ready, you rustlers!" he ground between his teeth. His words struck home. He gloated inwardly at the start the fellow could not conceal. On top of the man's remark concerning the mystery shot, here was another clue.

He sparred for time, casting about for some scheme.

"Is there anything to prevent you loosening these ropes until I bathe my head?" he stalled. "You've knocked me out twice . . . Unless you want to add another murder to your rustling, you'd better help me attend to this wound and give me a drink of water!"

The man eyed him sharply for an instant as if trying to read his mind.

"Don't get too mouthy with your guesses!" he snarled. "Some of them are liable to be close enough to the truth to get your yawp closed for keeps. Reckon if I did undo them ropes and let you wash that sore on your head, you'd only climb on your high hoss and try to make a break to get away."

"Fine chance of making a break while you're standing over me with a gun," Tobe countered, recognizing the truth in the fellow's warning and sensing that in his egotism — inflated by the helplessness of his prisoner — he could be swayed by a little pleading. "I'm not fool enough to commit suicide by trying to take your gun away from you."

The flattery served its purpose. Far better than he had even hoped.

"You're right there," the fellow conceded with an ugly leer. "Ain't many wallopers got any business tying up with me. And being as how you're acting sensible, I'll just get you some water."

Placing the lantern beside Tobasco, he crossed the cavern. Tobe's ears now caught the gurgle of water . . . Probably a spring rising in the floor of the cave . . . Then his captor was coming back with a dripping dipper. Cautiously he released Tobe's hands, stood, forty-five clutched at his hip, waiting for the youth to quench a feverish thirst and bathe his head.

The cooling water allayed the throbbing in Tobasco's head. When he had cleansed the wound as best he could, he pulled a kerchief from his pocket and tied it around his forehead in a crude bandage. His captor advanced to rebind his arms. Realizing that nothing was to be gained by attempting a break yet, he submitted without protest to the operation. Then, after the fellow

179

had gone back to settle down and resume his sleep, he stretched out and closed his eyes. But not to sleep, for his mind was working lightning fast.

After an infinity of time a heavy step sounded outside. Tobe's nerves went taut. He opened his eyes, watched the entrance, expecting to see the gangsters enter. The man who had given him the water was beside him quickly.

"We're having a visitor," he said in a lowered voice. "I'll have to stash you out of the way awhile." His gaze flew about the cave, centered on the farthest darkened corner. For an instant his face was revealed in the lantern light. Tobe could have sworn that it suddenly took on a pasty hue. But still, it might only have been his natural color. Yet it was obvious that he was perturbed about something. What, Tobe could not understand, unless possibly it was the arrival of the visitor.

"I can't hurt your caller with my hands and feet tied and unarmed," Tobasco remarked scornfully.

"I'll say you can't," the man returned grimly. "I don't reckon you or anyone else could hurt that walloper, if they was loose and toting a whole flock of guns. But I've got to get you out of the way just the same. It's the big boss — come to talk over business."

The announcement keyed Tobe's nerves to the highest pitch. Perhaps this visit might throw some light on the riddles crying for solution. He resolved to take any chance to overhear the conversation and discover, if possible, who the leader of the crew was. A movement

180

by his captor cut short the wild conjectures that started tumbling through his mind.

Stooping, the fellow seized him under the arms and started dragging him across the cave. Dropping him roughly to the floor, he strode back and returned with the lantern.

Tobe gazed around him in surprise. In the dancing light, he saw a partition of logs blocking the further corner of the cave. He watched the guard as he pried loose a great bar, raised it, and pulled open a door. From within came a rush of dank, putrid air. Tobasco shuddered, involuntarily recoiled from the inky blackness within. He shot a sidelong glance at his captor. The last vestige of color had left the fellow's face. It had taken on a deathly hue. The thought flashed to Tobe that fear — dread terror of something in this new cavern had unstrung his captor's nerve.

Fully aware of his hopeless plight, forced to the bitter realization that a struggle to keep from being placed in the awesome darkness would only bring another blow which, if it did not kill him, at least would preclude all chance of finding out who this leader was, he did not move a muscle in protest as the fellow rolled him inside. But the violent trembling of his captor's body added nothing to his fast-slipping assurance.

The door slammed shut. He heard the heavy bar fall into place. He was alone, engulfed in an impenetrable blackness that seemed to beat on his eardrums with its intensity.

CHAPTER
TWENTY-THREE

Arriving at the Lazy JP, Sheriff Joe Kazen and his weary possemen lost no time in routing out the cook and putting him to work preparing food. When it was ready they fell to it ravenously.

Having satisfied their hunger, they prowled around outside, impatiently awaiting orders. The sheriff paced around the yard, sunk in thought. After a time he called the men about him.

"Have any of you fellows got an idea?" he demanded abruptly.

"Not unless we ride up and see what's doing at the Horseshoe," Ivor Johnson suggested. "Mebbyso we can get a line on things from the cook up there and start all over again. He must know something that can give us some sort of a lead."

"That's a good idea," Kazen conceded. "We'll just do it." He motioned to one of the party to get their horses. When they were mounted, he galloped to the head of the column.

A short time later they rode into the Horseshoe yard expecting to find the place deserted by every one but the cook, as it had been the night before. Instead, to their amazement, Stevens and his men were at work tearing down the charred uprights of the fire-eaten ranchhouse. Kazen made no pretense at friendliness.

"Where did you come from?" he demanded, pinning down the foreman's shifting gaze.

"Where'd I come from?" Stevens straightened up to ask in surprise. "What do you mean?"

"Just what I said. Where did you come from? Where were you last night?"

"Had to throw a bunch of stuff onto them waterholes at the state section," Soapy answered. "We seen the fire and came back. But let me tell you right now. I'm gunning for that Pepper. I'll learn him to burn down my ranch-house!"

"Burn down your ranch-house?" Kazen blurted out. "Did Tobasco —"

"Sure he did it, the dirty, sneaking coyote!" Stevens blazed.

"How do you know?" the sheriff demanded.

"You heard him order me to move the house off his homestead, didn't you?" Stevens strode closer to eye the officer, his face twisted with rage. "He came right out in front of everybody and said the first thing I'd have to do was to move this house. As quick as it got dark and us jaspers pulled out what happened? The place burned down. If that ain't evidence enough to send him over the road I'd like to know what is. But you can just keep traveling. I don't need any help — I'll get him for it, don't worry!"

It was evident by Kazen's puzzled expression that the accusation had momentarily nonplused him. All too vividly did he recall Tobasco's words. They had been uttered in a threat. Yet deliberate arson, any underhanded thing, was not Tobasco's way. His puzzled gaze roved over the posse. The blank dismay registered on their faces showed plainly that the charge had left them speechless also.

"Huh!" The officer gave vent to his pet word when all others failed him.

Chuckwallow, however, quickly found his voice.

"You're a liar, Stevens!" he challenged. "Come up here!" He motioned to the homesteader who had told him of the fire. "Did Tobasco start that blaze?" he demanded.

"He did not!" The homesteader shook his head. "The Horseshoe ranch-house caught from the sparks from Pepper's shack."

"Huh!" cut in Kazen. "There you are, Soapy. Your charge didn't sound good to me. I've known Tobasco since he was knee-high to a grasshopper. And I never heard of him or any other Pepper doing anything like this. If he had burned you out it would have been while you were standing right here doing your damnedest to stop him — that's Tobasco. Why, there ain't an underhanded thing about that kid. He's playing 'em high, wide, and purty, above the table all the time, or else he don't play. Now who burned his cabin?"

Even in the face of this new evidence, Stevens was unperturbed. "How should I know who burned his damned shack?" he snapped. "We were down to the state section when it happened."

"Can you prove it?" Kazen shot in.

"Sure," was the surly reply. The foreman turned to his men, who were grouped about. "Didn't we take some critters to the state section last night, fellows?" They nodded. Just then the cook came up. Stevens faced him. "Didn't we get back and help you keep the flames from the bunkhouse and range?" The cook, too, nodded in affirmation. But it was obvious from his scowl he was in no mood to aid Soapy's cause if he could avoid it.

"You're plumb sure you don't know anything about how the fire started?" the officer persisted, plainly far from satisfied by Soapy's story.

"Only what the cook and Peggy told me. But they'd both lie to hide Pepper. I still think he did it on purpose. It's just about his size. I've got that big-headed walloper's number. He runs around here without no iron. He's afraid to pack one like a man, because he knows somebody will take it away from him and rap him over the head with it. His long suit is getting somebody arrested. Now I want to swear out a warrant for him and see how he likes it."

Chuckwallow jabbed his horse savagely with the rowels. It lunged forward. But Kazen intervened.

"Take 'er easy, Chuckwallow." Then to Stevens. "Sure I'll arrest Tobasco if you'll swear out a warrant. But we've got to find him first. Where's Peggy?"

"Turned over one of the bunkhouses to her," Soapy snarled. "Us fellows are bedded down in the barn."

Kazen blinked. This disclosure completely dumfounded him. That the girl was safe at the Horseshoe while they were peppering the Circle R believing her to be a prisoner, was beyond his comprehension.

"Fetch her out!" he ordered, convinced now that Stevens was lying and had walked into a trap he could not evade.

"Get her yourself," came the disconcerting answer. "You ain't crippled and I've got work to do."

Whirling his horse, the sheriff galloped to the bunkhouse. "Peggy!" he shouted.

To his amazement; the amazement of the posse, the girl appeared quickly.

"What is it?" she asked in a startled voice.

Kazen gulped, smothered an oath, stared at her in surprise. For the first time it struck him that perhaps Stevens was telling the truth and that he was not connected with the outrages. Yet, if that were so, the finger of guilt would point to Tobe. Joe Kazen clicked his teeth savagely at the thought.

"Where was you last night?" he demanded of the girl. "Where is Tobasco?"

She started to answer, but caught the eye of Stevens, who, in spite of his plea of having work to do, had followed.

"I don't know where Mr. Pepper is." She kept her gaze on the toe of her riding boot. "I —" Tears glistened on her lowered lashes. She struggled gamely against them.

"You what?" the officer encouraged.

"Oh, nothing. I —"

The sheriff lifted his dusty hat to scratch his head thoughtfully. Soapy's disarming answers and the

186

reappearance of the girl had increased his bewilderment until —

"Well, I'm damned!" he blurted out. "Wasn't you with Tobe when those wallopers attacked the Lazy JP?"

She nodded her head affirmatively.

"Then what happened?"

"We followed the gang to the hills. Mr. Pepper rode around to head them off. I went with him. They saw us. Rather than risk a fight with me along, Mr. — Tobe — threw down his gun. They —" Again she caught Stevens' eye and refused to continue.

"How'd you get back here?"

"One of our captors took me through the hills. We met Mr. Stevens and my men down by the state section. He turned me over to them and rode away."

"See?" chimed in Soapy gloatingly. "What did I tell you? I didn't even know she'd been molested until she told me. It was too late then to get a shot at the jasper who brought her back. We came on to the ranch to see if there was anything we could do to stop the fire."

The girl caught her breath sharply.

"Have you heard anything from To — Tobe?" she faltered.

"Don't even know where he is," Kazen growled. "Soapy, didn't you hear the shooting at the Lazy JP?"

"Sure, but it wasn't none of my business. I'm not under any contract to protect them jaspers. To hell with them. Let them go ahead and fight their own battles."

"Didn't you hear the shooting here at the Horseshoe when Tobasco was attacked and his shack burned?"

"Sure. But I couldn't tell where it was coming from. Gunfire after night is tricky . . . You know that, specially if there's a breeze. And I was clean down on the state section, I tell you!"

"Didn't you see the flames from Tobasco's shack?" Kazen kept pounding away.

Stevens never batted an eye.

"No! We must have been going the other way when it burned."

"But you must have smelled the smoke? Any cowhand would trail down smoke no matter what he —"

"Wind must of been against us," Soapy grunted.

"Didn't I warn you yesterday that if one of them homesteaders was molested I'd know where to come for the man who done it?"

"Yep!" snapped Soapy. "But you was taking in too much territory wasn't you? You've got to prove I did it before you can do anything, you know."

Checkmated at every turn, disarmed by the apparently frank answers, Kazen obviously was at his slow-wit's end. The foreman's alibi seemed air-tight. There was no denying his replies had the ring of truth. In spite of the dislike the fellow had always aroused within him, the officer was forced to admit for the moment that his suspicion was groundless. He looked at the girl. Something in her expression was pleading. Fear was stamped in her wide-eyed gaze. Yet she would not reveal what it was. He decided suddenly to talk it over with his posse before taking any rash action that might have embarrassing results.

188

"Come on, fellows," he said. "Let's ride over while we're here and see what they done to Tobasco's shack." He roweled past the charred ruins of the ranch-house, the others at his heels. Something prompted him to look back. The girl had fled back into the bunkhouse. Stevens had not moved, but stood watching them, an ugly, satisfied smile quirking his lips.

CHAPTER
TWENTY-FOUR

It took but a few minutes for Sheriff Kazen and the possemen to ride to the Horseshoe springs. But there was little to see; less on which to base a clue. The scene was one of utter desolation. The homestead shack was only a blackened heap. The lumber pile still smouldered. The brush was charred in a wide circle by the flames which had been checked by the spongy, water-soaked ground around the spring. The two tractors which had served a moving breastworks, and to which Tobe and his homesteaders no doubt owed their lives, were splattered with bullets. The strands of scorched rope, which bound the steering wheels in place, and which had held the improvised tanks to a straight course, were evidence of the youth's quick thinking.

The dilapidated cars were real junk now. Only the iron bands and wheel rims of the wagons remained.

The posse prowled about, trying to uncover something tangible on which to work. But the flames had obliterated anything that might have offered a clue to the identity of the besiegers. Under the rapid fire questioning of Kazen, the homesteaders, piece by piece, unfolded the story of the attack; pointed out where the unknown assailants had lain in the shelter of a dry wash

190

while they pumped lead at the party. But there were so many tracks it was impossible to follow them. They seemed to have come in from the direction opposite the Horseshoe. The officer and his posse were more and more perplexed.

Almost two hours had elapsed before a thorough survey was completed. Returning to the ruins, Kazen walked around thoughtfully, clearly at a loss where to begin in an attempt to place the blame. So far as he knew, no one but the Horseshoe outfit would have any reason to burn the shack. The ill feeling between Tobasco and Stevens was, in itself, motive enough on which to base a theory. Again there was Tobe's threat — voiced in Kazen's presence — that the first move Soapy would be forced to make was that of the ranch-house. Then there were the homesteaders' claims that sparks from the blazing shack had ignited the Horseshoe. But then, as Pepper men, they could be expected to say nothing else.

Much as he disliked to, the sheriff was forced to admit that suspicion rested upon Tobasco as strongly as it did Stevens. And while he never had known Tobe to do an underhand thing, it was well within the realm of possibility that destruction of his shack might have caused him to retaliate as Soapy had charged.

There Kazen ran against a stone wall with his conjectures. He shifted his line of reasoning. The cook, he thought, might tell something if he would. But knowing Stevens, he realized he never could pry a word from either the cook or the Horseshoe men until they were away from the foreman. That Peggy, too, knew something she had not told, he was positive. But fear had sealed her lips, too. One by one he recalled Soapy's answers to his questions, trying to pick some flaw in them.

"He's a liar?" he blurted out with a suddenness that sent his startled horse lunging back on the reins. "Since when have they begun driving cows at night on the Chimney Rock range?"

"Sure he is, if you're referring to our good friend Mr. Stevens," Johnson chimed in. "I had a hunch back yonder when he was answering your questions so damned all-fired quick. His alibi was just a little too danged good to get across if you'd ask me."

"Driving critters at night ain't so strange as it sounds on Chimney Rock or any other range," Chuckwallow put in. "Especially when it's as dry as it's been and cows are as thirsty as ours. You don't want to overlook the fact that his stuff ain't got no water neither, since Tobe moved in here. And it's been powerful hot today. Mebby he waited until dark so's they could make the trip without ga'nting 'em up too much. And while I think of it, Joe; all our critters are down yonder on that State section."

"Let 'em stay there!" Kazen growled, sidetracked again by Chuckwallow's argument. "Tobe told me he was going to tear down that division fence. He's plumb within the law. We've got plenty to worry about besides them critters. When the Horseshoe gets a legal fence around the waterholes, then make them drive your cattle out. If they don't want stock in there it's up to them to build a fence. But I ain't got time to think about stock right now. The rustling has almost drove me loco. This here burning shacks and houses is going to drive me locoer . . . And gunfights and raids . . . We've got to do something. We can't be setting here like a bunch of fence posts!"

He climbed into the saddle and wheeled his horse.

"Where are you going?" Johnson demanded.

"To arrest Soapy!" was the decisive reply as the sheriff started back toward the Horseshoe.

"What for?"

"Dunno! But I'm going to arrest him if I have to get him to yank a gun on me."

They followed in silence, presently to pull up at the bunkhouses in a cloud of dust. The punchers working about the ruins where they had left them, did not look up. Kazen looked around for Stevens. He was not in sight. The cook detached himself from the group and came forward.

"Where's Soapy?" the sheriff demanded.

"Him and Peggy rode off before you was hardly out of sight," the cook growled.

"Hell's Bobcats!" Kazen exploded. "Now I know there's something snaky about that hombre. And we let him slip out of our hands. Which way did they go?"

"Toward the Lazy JP. And they was riding like hell. Peggy didn't want to go, but he made her. Hold on, just a minute," as Kazen dragged his horse about. The cook sidled nearer and lowered his voice, watching the punchers, who suddenly had quit their work, and were coming toward him.

"Soapy or any of them wallopers would kill me in a minute if they knowed I told. But they didn't drive no cows to the state section last night. Stevens is the one as shot hell out of Tobasco's homestead and burned it. The sparks caught the Horseshoe like that fellow —" indicating the homesteader — "said. Peggy was locked in her room inside. Stevens locked her in there. Tobasco and me caught her just when she jumped from the second story window. He —" He broke off suddenly as the Horseshoe men came within earshot. "It wasn't so hard to stop the flames," he changed the subject quickly in tones loud enough for all to hear. "You see, the fellows came back right after they got started good and we all pitched in and knocked the devil right out of the fire."

Kazen had heard enough before the inconsequential fill-in . . . His gun leaped from its holster and swept the dumfounded crew. "Throw down them irons!" he grated. "I had a hunch you hoot-owlers were the ones as burned that shack. But I couldn't get the goods on you. Now snake up your horses and climb aboard. You're under arrest, every one of you!"

Oaths sprang to the lips of the men, who wheeled furiously on the cook.

"That's all right, you dirty, sneaking coyotes!" the cook flared. "I told that Stevens, when he made me go with you, I'd get even. I never squealed on you hombres before, and I wouldn't now if you hadn't started playing Soapy's dirty game. Now you take the medicine that always comes to tinhorns!" He stood spread-legged, glaring balefully at the sullen punchers, who had thrown down their guns.

"Get a move on!" ordered Kazen. "We ain't got no time to waste monkeying with you wallopers. There's other things to do. But don't think for a minute we won't make you come clean with all you know before we get through with you. Here," to half a dozen of the posse, "you fellows are deputies. Ride herd on these coyotes. Head them back to Bigtrails. Have the prosecuting attorney lock them up. I'll lay just plenty of charges against them when I get to town."

He collected the firearms the men had thrown down, and distributed them to the grim-faced possemen, whom he knew would see the crew into Bigtrails without a hitch. He waited with impatience until the Horseshoe men had saddled their horses, were mounted and on their way. Then, with the remainder of his party, he was gone toward the Lazy JP in a thunder of hoofs, the grinning cook looking after them.

CHAPTER
TWENTY-FIVE

Back in the cavern, the terrifying sensation of absolute silence; silence that seems tangible, the like of which is to be encountered only deep in the bowels of the earth. An overwhelming, suffocating silence that creates a panic in the strongest heart, set cold chills to racing up and down Tobasco's spine.

He lay motionless for several moments in the new cave into which his captor had dragged him, his labored breath rasping on his ear-drums which had become so sensitive in the oppressive stillness that it seemed as though the slightest sound would burst them. He strove to pierce the impenetrable blackness that blotted out his surroundings. But that blackness was as deep and horrible as the silence itself.

Taking firm hold on himself presently, he rolled up alongside the partition and wedged his ear against the rough logs. The sound of his own movements seemed to relieve the nerve-racking tension. Faintly, through the 'dobe chinking of the partition, came to him a voice raised loud in anger.

Tobasco's nerves went taut again. He jerked with muscular violence, gritted his teeth on the stunning impotence that suddenly assailed him.

That voice belonged to Soapy Stevens!

Soapy Stevens was the big boss of the gang!

If that was true — and it was, else why was Stevens in the cavern — Soapy was the mysterious owner of the Circle R; the man who had stocked the range with gunmen posing as homesteaders!

When the roar of his own hot blood had stopped sluicing in his ears, he listened again. His breath seemed deafening as he tried to hold it, his heart pounded audibly. But no other sound came to his straining ears. Stevens either had left or was speaking now in guarded tones. With bated breath, Tobasco waited, but no further word rewarded his vigil. Giving up presently, he eased his cramped position and set about in an attempt to solve the riddles.

Thought of Peggy flashed to his mind. But now that he had discovered Stevens' secret, he knew the gangsters would not dare to harm the wife of their leader. Now he realized the reason for the quick cessation of firing when he had mentioned her name at the time of his capture, when they had ridden out in search of the attackers of the Lazy JP. Those assailants had been fearful a chance shot might wound her.

One by one the problems stalked before him in grim array. He pondered over the brand — Circle R! He twisted it about in his mind, mentally placed it beside the Lazy JP and Horseshoe.

"Circle R!" he blurted out hoarsely, startled by the echoing whispers of his own voice that beat back at him from every corner. "And to think — as good a cowman as Dad was and he couldn't see it — and Chuckwallow.

A brand only for convenience!" He suddenly had hit upon the secret. By converting the P in the Lazy JP into an R, using the lower part of the J as a quarter circle, then enclosing the whole brand in a circle the result was a Circle R. Running the Horseshoe was still a simpler matter. By forming the R with the Horseshoe as the loop and placing a circle about it the same results were obtainable.

This then was the mystery of the Circle R! Obviously a melting pot of thievery, preying on Lazy JP and Horseshoe herds alike. The occasional slaughtered beef, the constant cry of rustlers was a subterfuge to divert suspicion and throw the authorities off the trail. And Stevens was the leader of the lot. Playing a dual rôle — half owner of the Horseshoe, stealing from himself — and breaking Peggy for the Circle R.

With the knowledge that he was now in possession of their secret, he cursed himself grimly for not having thought of it before — it was so utterly simple. He realized more than ever the need for speed in his fight for freedom, but buried within the tomb, he was powerless to bring them to justice. He cast about wildly for some way to rid himself of the fetters before he was dragged back into the other cavern under the watchful eyes of the guards. He could only stare helplessly into the awesome blackness. Yet sheer desperation urged him on. In spite of the throbbing wound on his head, his mind suddenly became alert and active. Only his muscles refused to obey. They were sore and logy, rebelling at further punishment.

Determined, however, to do something, goaded to action by the awful silence, he rolled across the damp, rock-littered floor, feeling his way cautiously with his head as he went, lest he plunge to death in some subterranean pit concealed by the darkness.

Presently he bumped against the rear wall of the cave. Instinctively he knew that the roof was just above him, that this new cavern was smaller and lower than the one from which he had been brought. He ran his cheek as far as he was able up the side wall. It was smooth sandstone; did not offer even a projecting point on which to saw the bonds.

Thought of a jack-knife in his pocket gave him momentary hope. But, shackled as he was, he might as well have been without it. He lay back panting, spent and dizzy by his efforts, a sudden victim to the pangs of hunger and fatigue.

Then suddenly, from out of the tomb-like silence about him flashed an idea. With it came new strength. Squirming about, he placed his feet against the wall. By bridging his body, then pushing himself forward on his shoulders, he succeeded in raising them. Using the back of his head and his fingers bound behind him for propellers, he walked toward the wall on his shoulders pushing up his feet inch by inch. Several times he all but lost his balance in the awkward position, but at last he stood on his shoulders, his feet braced against the wall.

Followed a breathless period of fear and exultation. He shook himself as much as he dared without toppling over. With a jingle, amplified a hundred times by his sensitive ears, the contents of his trouser pockets slid down to the ground. He waited, expecting the noise to bring his captors on a run. A few moments and he breathed easier. No sound came from the entrance.

The new position temporarily relieved the aching of his muscles. He held it for a time. One of those singular inane flashes that bob from nowhere in a time of danger, came to his mind. He recalled the mistrust and coldness his riding breeches had aroused among the Lazy JP riders — ladies' breeches the cowboys had called them sneeringly. In spite of the seriousness of his predicament, he smiled. The riding breeches with high, slit pockets, which easily disgorged their contents, might yet be the means of saving his life. Had he been hampered with the chaps of which the punchers were so proud, the jack-knife would still be buried deep in the leather and beyond reach.

Having caught his breath, which rasped in his parched throat with the exertion, he worked his feet down the wall as quietly as he raised them.

Then came the problem of locating the knife in the darkness. With his hands bound, able to feel only within a limited space, beneath his body, the task seemed well nigh impossible. There was but a slight hope for the success of his scheme. But that hope occupied his mind, spurred his brain to alertness and kept him from brooding over his plight.

After an infinity of time, lengthened by a constant fear that his captors would come for him, his fingers closed over the jack-knife. He broke his nails to the quick trying to open the blade behind his back. After several vain attempts he succeeded. Rolling over, he picked up the knife between his teeth and squirmed about in the darkness, seeking some hole or opening large enough to hold it upright.

Forced to drive his sore and aching muscles to action, the time it took to move from rock to rock, work his body across each one and feel their surfaces, seemed endless. Unless his captors had had others in the dungeon before him and knew of a certainty there was no escape, it was odd that they would leave him alone so long. With that thought came another. Now that he had a slim chance to rid himself of the bonds, he grew fearful that they had decided to let him remain a prisoner in the evil-smelling cave.

Weird notions persisted in tormenting him. Nerves, he told himself as he threshed about on the damp floor. He wondered about Stevens. What he already had learned drove from his mind all else. Then — his bleeding fingers, clawing at a sharp-edged stone beneath him, had encountered a crevice!

Steeling himself against the pain, he twisted over and dropped the knife from between his teeth upon the rock. Sitting down and bracing his heels in the dirt floor, he pushed himself across it backwards. When he had worked himself clear over, he made a bridge of his body. He groped around beneath him for the knife and found it. Digging in his heels to avoid a chance slip that would plunge it into his back, he raised himself on his heels and head and placed the handle upright in the fissure. Carefully he dragged the fetters that bound his wrists along the keen blade.

A sickening wave of failure enveloped him. The knife slipped from its insecure position and clattered down the side of the rock to the ground. He smothered the exclamation of disappointment that sprang to his lips. But there was no alternative. His one hope of ridding himself of those fetters lay in the knife. He started anew the heart-breaking task. Again and again he gritted his teeth and rolled his aching body over in search of the knife. With maddening regularity it defied his efforts and slid from the cleft. At last he succeeded in wedging it in tightly. He held his breath as he ran the fetters along the sharp edge.

The strands parted! His hands were free! He could scarcely hold back a shout of joy.

CHAPTER
TWENTY-SIX

With his first move toward a dash for freedom successful, Tobasco realized more than ever the greater need for haste. Bound and helpless he would not have had a chance for escape had his captors returned. But now, in spite of the protest of his weary aching body, he had made for himself a chance worth taking.

Again the knife had fallen to the dirt floor. Leaning over, he ran his fingers along the ground in search of it.

A shudder racked him. His face became fixed with a cold, death-like pallor that drove out the blood and set it crashing in the wound, on his head. He experienced his first flash of sickening fear in a wave of nausea that left his brain spinning.

His fingers had closed over bones . . . They felt like the bones of a hand!

Completely unnerved, he bolted upright to a sitting posture, the horror of the moment almost unendurable. Until his body ceased its violent trembling he sat rigid. Then with awkward fingers pulled a match from the pocket of his shirt. Turning over and lying flat on the rock to shield the flame with his body, he struck it. Blinded even by its tiny light for a moment, he waited until the glare was less blinding. Then he looked. His gaze became one of stupefaction.

Beside him stretched a skeleton!

Something shiny caught his eye. Before he thought, he reached for it. The match flickered out. He jerked his hand away, far more fearful of this grim reminder of tragedy in the darkness than in the light. In his palm lay the shiny object he had stripped unintentionally from the bony finger. It was a ring! Not caring to feel the cold bones to replace it, nor daring to strike another match, he rammed it into his pocket.

As he hesitated, there came to him an explanation of the nervousness of the guard when he had approached the cave. The pasty gray of his face had not been a natural color. It had been caused by terror — stark terror of the unknown that any cadaver arouses within everyone. That guard knew the gruesome secret of the inner cavern. And, knowing it, he had been reluctant even to open the door.

The uneasiness that had gripped him since being thrown into the darkness grew to a haunting fear with the shock of the ghastly discovery. He made frantic haste to locate the knife. No longer did he dread the guard's return. He welcomed it in preference to being alone. Nothing in the outer cave could compare to the utter loneliness which assailed him.

Came another thought to torment him; that a fate similar to that which had befallen this victim of the blackness and awful silence might be in store for him. He resolved at any cost not to endure the torture and the agony this other must have suffered before death closed the eyes long sightless in the darkness. That the man — it must have been a man he decided — might not have died within the tomb did not occur to him. But if it had, it would have lessened his apprehension not one whit.

After an infinity of frantic groping he found the knife. With a strength of which he did not think himself capable, he severed the bonds about his ankles in a single stroke. Tearing off the pieces of rope with trembling fingers, he closed the knife and jammed it into his pocket. Staggering to his feet, he lurched blindly in the direction he thought the entrance to be.

But the blackness had destroyed his sense of direction. Panic seized him. He was milling about in a circle. He stopped; strove to collect his wits, only to find himself beset with a million haunting fancies. Try as he would, he failed utterly to drive the picture of the skeleton from his mind. Pity for that unknown man who had met so tragic an end filled his heart. With that pity came a flaming anger that further unstrung his frayed and quivering nerves. If the villainous crew — Soapy Stevens' Circle R gunmen and rustlers, he now knew them to be — had been guilty of such fiendish treatment, the worst punishment that the courts of justice could mete out was pitifully weak to pay them back in kind. For the first time, since as a reckless boy he had unstrapped his Colt and become an advocate of law and order, that law in which he placed implicit faith seemed ineffectual.

In the olden days, a gun to him had meant only splitting a second with some swaggering trigger-fanner.

It was a way to bring to a sudden end all small disputes. The flaming steel had lured him with the sense of security it gave; had given him a powerful mastery over men who lacked the suppleness of wrist to draw with his own lightning speed.

But now he better understood why and how his father, Chuckwallow, and all the rest of the old-timers had learned to carry and insist upon their Colts. It was their law — swift and deadly — and made especially to blaze out justice for such heinous crimes as this; crimes of which the law of Rangeland took no note, was unable to solve or was ignorant of entirely.

Scarcely realizing what he was doing, he was groping along the walls in search of the partition. The ordeal and the aftermath of haunting fancies had sapped his strength and drained his courage. It seemed that even his reason would give under the strain unless he could get out of the suffocating darkness quickly. Stark terror of the infernal stillness, the gruesome skeleton, the waning hope of seeing daylight, made him frantic.

Then to add to this torment came the thought of Peggy. That she, too, might be incarcerated in some horrible dungeon as dark and silent as this, drove him to the verge of madness. Came before his mind the mask-like face of Stevens — backed by eyes which were steely and merciless. Stevens had made good the threats he had taken so lightly. Soapy Stevens had finally played the trump card. He was a helpless prisoner in the power of the Horseshoe foreman. Grimly, now, he admitted to himself the fear that he was locked forever in the cavern. If he could just get word to

206

Chuckwallow, to Kazen — to anyone — but the hope died as it was born.

After an infinity of time he bumped against the logs of the partition. He leaned against them panting, fighting to recover his breath, get control of his singing nerves. This lifeless barrier between him and freedom gave him strength for the moment. He straightened up. Impending danger jerked coherence to his swirling mind.

The heavy bar outside the door had shifted. He could hear it scraping on the log as it raised. He waited, tense, motionless.

A breath of air, foul-smelling, but still far better than that which he was breathing, swept in. All the pent-up fear, the torture of the passing moments, the terror of the ghastly discovery centered in a cold fury which left him steady, cool, and eager to assume any risk, death itself, to break for liberty. His heart and soul cried out for vengeance; vengeance for the skeleton, or the murder of his father, vengeance for the capture of Peggy . . . For every act of which he suddenly knew the gang to be guilty.

Through throbbing ears he heard the voice of the guard.

"Where are you?"

He was thinking quickly, cunningly weighing his chances. It was the old Tobasco now . . . The years had rolled back . . . It was the Tobasco who fought at the drop of a hat and reveled in the fighting.

Again the guard's voice.

"Roll over here and I'll give you a better place to bed down!"

Tobasco's nerves were singing with the tension. If he could but reach the outer cave without his shackles, he felt fit to defy the two, the whole crew if necessary. Stooping, he picked up a large rock, drew further into the shadows, and emitted a piteous groan.

His ruse worked.

"He's dying!" shouted the fellow hoarsely. Tobasco heard his companion running to his side. "Get the lantern! Let's snake him out. I don't want to go into that damned — graveyard!"

Realizing that light spelled doom for his plans, Tobasco leaped forward, struck the man over the head with the rock. Without a sound he crumpled forward in the youth's arms. Pulling him into the darkness, Tobasco seized his gun from its holster. Before the other could enter with the lantern, he leaped into the outer cavern.

"Throw down your gun!" he shouted hoarsely.

The man wheeled. Tobe got one full look at his face. Then the lantern crashed to the ground, flickered out. The cave was in darkness. That one look had been enough. His captor was the stranger of the Goldbug; the stranger with *two fingers missing* on his right hand!

CHAPTER
TWENTY-SEVEN

Poignant silence settled over the cavern; silence far more deadly than that he had experienced in the inner chamber. But now it went unheeded. A grim and terrible mood enveloped Tobasco. Forgotten, for the moment, was the memory of his own experiences. He only knew that somewhere in the black void before him crouched the man his father had accused of murdering him. If, as he suspected, he was the fugitive mentioned in Kazen's circular, then he was no coward, but a relentless killer, who, now that he was fighting for his life, would stop at nothing.

For the first time in four years, Tobasco thrilled to the feel of cold steel in his hand. Again it was part of him, his means of claiming justice, wreaking vengeance in spite of the precepts that had taught him otherwise. Gone in a twinkling were the tenets of the law. He was a gunman like his father, like Chuckwallow, like every other old-timer. His own law at his hip, easing further back into the shadows, waiting, clear-eyed, nerveless, for his foe to move. The pantomime was eerie, stark and deadly; the darkness unpierced, save for the wan rays of a dying sun filtering through the 'dobe-chunked logs at the entrance.

209

Minutes dragged on, minutes without breath or motion; tense minutes that found him struggling to stifle a wild desire to leap forth and deliberately draw the other's fire. Reckless passion that knew no fear keyed his strumming nerves.

He kicked the wall, then leaped aside. A jet of flame stabbed the darkness! The cave roared with the echo. It had given him his opening. The bullet had barely splattered against the wall at his side when his gun spoke. In that orange pencil of powder flame that laced the gloom he caught sight of the other's face . . . An ugly face, unshaven, livid, leering.

Again a spurt of fire. More deafening reverberations. The acrid smoke eddying ceilingward burned Tobasco's eyes and nose. He waited, motionless. His quick ear caught a slithering sound across the cave. Silence! He jerked violently from his gunman's crouch, shook off the deadening lethargy of passion. In a half dozen swift strides he had crossed the cave, was before the door. He kicked it open. He stood for a moment, blinded, looked down at the still figure prostrate in the path of light. Stooping quickly, he ripped open the front of the shirt.

A naked woman was tattooed on the fellow's chest!

He tore the gun from the limp fingers; unbuckled the cartridge belt and strapped it about his own waist. Then he left — left in a single bound that took him to the ledge trail winding a dizzy height above the valley, one hot-barreled gun clutched in his hand, another swung at his hip.

The narrow path lay straight and without danger to the eyes which still saw red. At the moment he had one

210

regret — that a flash of passion had swept him back unyielding to days when he reveled in the whine of flaming lead. He cast it aside; strode on, head up, nostrils flaring, weakness and fatigue submerged in deadly anger.

A sentry pacing the space where the ledge trail joined the hills, sighted him. Two shots cracked one on the other. Stepping across the body which lodged against a tree to dangle awkwardly over the dizzy precipice, Tobasco went on.

Sound of the shots brought the gang swarming in. Both Tobasco's forty-fives now went to spitting lead. He plowed through. Shaking his head like an enraged bull, he dodged to shelter behind a giant pine. Oblivious to the whistling bullets he worked his way from tree to tree. He risked a glance over his shoulder. The Chimney Rocks rose stark and ugly beyond the timber. Once he gained the barren pile, he could hold off an army.

Out of range of their Colts, he sprinted, refilling his forty-five as he ran. Looking back he saw the men dragging horses from a barn built in the hillside. He bowled straight ahead. He could hear the thunder of pursuing hoofs coming closer, closer. A bullet whined past his ear. The song of hate it sang turned his soul to ice.

Then of a sudden he was conscious that the hoof-beats had ceased. He spun about. The gang had turned back. He swept the prairies, aflame with color in the late afternoon sun. A large party of mounted men were bearing down upon him from the north.

The sudden flight of the gangsters told him that the approaching party were friends. He tried to shout to them, but the words choked in his parched throat. Now that help was at hand, he was aware of a tormenting thirst. Fierce hunger assailed him. The wound on his head, which he had forgotten in the excitement, began pounding like a sledge. A sense-deadening weariness was creeping over him. His legs moved mechanically. His muscles were numb from exertion, responding only to his greatest effort.

He gained the shelter of the Chimney Rocks. The prairies suddenly began to sway and dance grotesquely. He struggled to ward off the descending cloud of darkness. He staggered back, tried frantically to signal the horsemen who only continued south at a gallop. Then he pitched down headlong, the world tumbling crazily about him.

A feeling of impending danger aroused him. He drew further into a niche in the Chimney Rocks, raised up weakly and peered around. Two riders had cleared the timber from the direction of the Circle R and were coming toward him at a mad gallop. He dragged a trembling hand across his burning blood-shot eyes. One of those riders was a woman — Peggy. A gigantic weight rolled from his shoulders with knowledge that she was safe. A spurt of hot blood threw strength into his fatigue-numbed muscles.

For her companion was Soapy Stevens!

He got to his knees, slunk further into the shelter, fighting to pull together his quivering nerves. The two were almost upon him. He could hear them talking. He

212

found himself hoping the party of horsemen, which he took to be Kazen and a posse, would not swing back. The fingers that closed about the butt of one of his guns were steady, strong as steel.

He watched the two as they dismounted. Soapy was pleading earnestly. Peggy stood with fists clenched, her face pale with rage.

"But you didn't tell me that when I married you!" she flashed. "You're a coward and — a — liar!"

Tobasco's eyes centered with fascination on the square of white in Stevens' pocket directly over his heart. It loomed a perfect target. He fought to master his impatience.

"I wanted to get hold of the Lazy JP!" came Soapy's gruff voice. "I knew if I could lease that state section with the water I could drive them out of the country."

"But you didn't," flared the girl. "You only succeeded in setting the range on fire with war — war, murder —"

"It's that damned Pepper in his dude pants!" retorted Stevens savagely. "You're stuck on him. I didn't figure he had brains enough to fight back. Then, again, you didn't tell me our water-holes were open to entry . . . It's a bad break of luck, the ranch-house burning down and all. But now I've got that damned Pepper where I want him. He won't bother you — he won't be able to bother anybody no more!"

"You deserve everything you got!" she blazed recklessly. "I wish Uncle Jake hadn't made that will. Then I wouldn't have been an unwilling party to your crimes. I was forced into this marriage. You dare not deny it!" She advanced threateningly, her black eyes flecked with points of flame. "That foolish will which made us partners if I married you — penniless if I did not. And I thought Uncle Jake loved me. It's too — too —" Anger loosed a flood of tears.

"Bawl!" he told her brutally. "You don't regret that will any more than I do. You've never been my wife — you've been a stranger, hampering me at every turn — because you loved that Pepper — your sweetheart!"

Tobasco restrained himself with a tremendous effort. He hung on to the girl's next words.

"I do love him!" she admitted. "I've always loved him. I always will love him. He's a man. You're not. Who brought all these strangers you call homesteaders in? Who attacked Tobe's cabin? Who surrounded the Lazy JP? Where is he now? You'll turn him loose or I'll tell everything I know!"

Cold fury twisted Stevens' face. "You try it. I burned his cabin. The Circle R gang surrounded the Lazy JP and every one of them is my men. I own that outfit. That's where they took your city friend. Then to our cave up yonder. That's where I stopped when the men guarded you. They've fixed him by now —"

Tobasco laid his gun on the ground, rammed his hands into his pockets to keep from firing. His fingers came in contact with the ring he had taken from the clammy fingers of the skeleton in the cave. Gingerly he drew it forth. Blank amazement crossed his face. It was a signet ring. The interwoven initials "JE" stared up at him.

214

The girl's voice jerked him away from the new thoughts that came tumbling into his mind.

"If anything has happened to him, you'll pay —"

The thud of hoofs cut short his reply. Having sighted the two, Kazen was charging down upon the Chimney Rocks. Tobasco cursed the sheriff under his breath for his interference. Shaking off his weakness, he bounded from his shelter, faced the startled pair just as the posse thundered up.

A shout broke from the Lazy JP punchers. Tobasco paid no heed. He held Stevens' eye locked in a steady gaze.

Peggy recoiled, clutched at the air for support. Her mind had halted. Tobasco was coming, crouched, his face set in hard lines, the muscles at the corners of his jaws twitching; his eyes narrowed to slits. She shot a glance at Stevens. His body was rigid. His lips were braced in a thin white line, but not through fear.

"Get back! Get back!" roared Kazen. "Peggy!" Spurring his horse to her side, he seized the girl and dragged her into his saddle. She felt a sickening sense of sinking down. Then she dared a look. Her heart stood stock still. Only a few paces separated the glaring men.

Somewhere in the posse someone gasped, a whistling sound that burst harshly on the piercing stillness.

A shot rang out; another echoed its report. Then she seemed to sink into darkness.

She groped back to consciousness. She was lying down. Someone was supporting her head, brushing the hair from her brow. She dreaded to look.

Then a voice. It was Chuckwallow, speaking from a great distance.

"I knowed you'd come to some day, kid. You was the only man that ever hit these parts who could split a second on the trigger with Soapy!"

"But this paper we took from Soapy's shirt pocket you drilled plumb through the middle," came the puzzled tone of Kazen. "It's old Jake's will. And to think the dirty cur forged the other one just to get Peggy to marry him — so he could claim an interest in the ranch when she owned it all along — and he killed Jake in cold blood . . . That beats me!"

The words brought Peggy struggling to her elbow to meet the calm gaze of Tobe, who held her nerve-racked form.

"Uncle Jake — murdered!" she gasped weakly. "Who —"

"Stevens!" Kazen told her bluntly. "Your uncle never died in the East. He's up yonder in a cave — dead. Tobe found his ring. See!"

Then she was staring with dull eyes at a signet ring on which a "JE" was intertwined. No need to ask to whom it belonged. She had seen it on her uncle's finger since she was a child. She turned it over in her hand, and sank back with a moan. The world seemed falling down. Uncle Jake — murdered — by Stevens!

Kazen turned to Tobe.

"And to think just after I'd got that circular, you discovered Two-Finger Brown had killed your paw. He's the one as took a crack at you that night for running him out of town, I'm betting. Where does that cave lay, Tobasco? How do you know it was him? Did he have that naked lady tattooed on his chest?"

Tobe must have nodded. She did not hear him speak.

Came Kazen's voice again.

"My God! This ain't Soapy Stevens! It's Cimarron George! Look, Tobasco. It's Cimarron George. He's got that naked lady tattooed on his chest too!"

Then the possemen stirred themselves. She could hear their horses moving about, champing impatiently on the bits.

She dragged her swirling mind back to catch Kazen's words. "You take Peggy back to the Lazy JP, Tobasco. We'll ride on. There's a heap of work to do yet. But now Two-Finger Brown and Cimarron George are both gone, whipping their hired gunmen in that cave won't be no big trick. Circle R? Sure you figured it out right. It's just a blind brand — picked on purpose to run Lazy JP's and Horseshoe's without blotching. Home-steaders? Homesteaders hell! They're everyone of them gunmen — paid off from Peggy's money, and the poor little cuss not knowing a thing about it all the time."

Chuckwallow broke in. She felt the figure holding her close move.

"We're for you, Tobasco," came the foreman's broken voice. "You're all man even . . . Well, dude pants and puttees and all!"

Tobasco spoke for the first time.

"I'd better go to jail, Joe!" She could feel his heart thumping against her shoulder. "I guess I'm still a lead-slinging, senseless fool."

"Go to jail?" bawled Kazen. "For shooting Two-Finger Brown and Cimarron George? When there are reward notices as long as your arm out for them dead or alive? For shooting any of them Circle R hombres? Not on your life you ain't going to jail. You was toting your gun in the name of the law. I'll leave it to any of the fellows. Didn't I make him a deputy sheriff in front of Mason and his cavalry — even if he didn't know it? Besides, I've got the jail full of Horseshoe hombres! And I'll have it even fuller with Circle —"

A chorus of shouts. Peggy thrilled. somehow the knowledge took the sting from her heart. She moved her arm.

Then it was around his neck. Her lips were on his.

"Tobe," she whispered. "At last I have the right to say it . . . I love you!"